WILD ALPINE

TYSON WILD BOOK SIXTY ONE

TRIPP ELLIS

1

It was bad news from the moment I heard her sobbing, frantic voice on the other end of the line.

But it just kept getting worse.

As Madison told me the terrible story, her voice deteriorated, her throat tightened—the sheer panic intensifying.

That horrible sensation twisted in my stomach—to know that someone I care about was in agony and not being able to do anything about it. No words I could say would comfort her or take away the pain. The only thing I could do was assure her I would do my best to resolve the situation.

My sister hadn't spoken to me in years, and understandably so. Due to my line of work, people close to me often became targets. If someone wanted to hurt me, the best way to do it was to go after the people I cared about. And there were a lot of people out there that wanted to hurt me.

Madison wanted nothing to do with me. I couldn't blame her. Not in her situation. The stakes were higher for her now.

She had gone *no contact*.

Not a word in several years.

I had a vague idea of where she might be but no specific details. There were no Christmas cards. No phone calls. No messages of *Happy Birthday*. I existed in a world without her, leaving a vacant hole.

I wanted nothing more than to repair our relationship.

After my parents' death, we were all we had left. My only blood relative. JD was family—there was no doubt about it. But to lose contact with Madison cut deep. Hearing her in distress wasn't the way I wanted our reunion to go down.

I had gone from one extreme to the other. When she first called, I was in the Texas Hill Country, having wrapped up a case. We were en route to Austin—the band had a gig on Sixth Street. JD stayed behind with the guys to live up to his obligation, and I took the next plane out. My journey took me from the unusual November heat wave in Texas to the frigid temperatures of Colorado.

I had chartered a *Slipstream G-750*. No lines, no waiting, no security checks. The sleek, luxury craft sliced through the air, and I spent the entire flight on edge. Despite the buttery soft leather seats, the elegant appointments, and the cheery cabin attendants, I was a ball of stress.

The pilot adjusted our airspeed as we began our descent into the valley.

I glanced out the window at majestic snow-covered peaks that stabbed the gray sky, piercing a veil of clouds. It was almost dusk. This was a far cry from the Florida Keys and a sharp contrast to the blistering Texas sun. It dawned on me that I hadn't prepared for a winter trip.

The blood rushed to my head as the plane angled toward the tarmac below. Wisps of clouds streaked past the windows. Finally, the wheels barked against the runway, and the plane shimmied for a moment, then settled.

We taxied to the terminal at the FBO, anticipation tingling my skin. I wanted to hit the ground running. This was no ordinary case. This was personal.

The cute flight attendants smiled and waved, their eyes sparkling as I disembarked. "I hope everything works out," the blonde said.

"Me too."

The blonde had given me her number. I didn't know if I'd have the opportunity to use it. This wasn't a recreational trip.

The biting air hit my skin, raising goosebumps as tall as skyscrapers. This was December in the Colorado Rockies— not the place for shorts and a T-shirt.

I hustled into the terminal, found a gift shop, and bought a puffer jacket and a pair of sweatpants. I figured I could buy more clothes when I got to my destination. My roller case was full of light wardrobe items that had already been worn for a week and needed a wash.

The small airport was just big enough for regional jets and private planes. The resorts in the area were the playground of the rich and famous, and no expense was spared to accommodate their every desire. Sit in the FBO long enough, and you'd see celebrities come and go—movie stars, pop icons, politicians.

Fortunately, I was able to get a rental car on such short notice—an Ice Cap White RAV4. I drove up the twisty mountain road that led to Alpine Park. This was the only way in or out of the ski town. There was regular helicopter service from the FBO to the luxury resort—the preferred method of travel for the elite. I figured it might come in handy to have my own vehicle.

The mountain pass curved through minty evergreens, sheer cliffs, and monumental peaks. A sparkling creek ran along the roadway. The air was crisp and clean here. Not a hint of smog. Just the smell of the unspoiled outdoors and spicy evergreens.

The terrain was beautiful but treacherous. Wander off the beaten path, and there was a host of dangers that awaited. Steep cliffs, vicious wildlife, and deep snow.

Founded as a mining camp during the silver boom of the 1880s, Alpine Park withered after the bust. With the collapse of the silver market, the population declined to a few hundred. Things turned around when the ski boom came along. Soon, the landscape was dotted with luxury accommodations, and the population grew to over 7,000, which swells during ski season.

If you're brave and willing to make the hike, you can see some of the abandoned silver mines. But stepping into one of the dank, dark shafts is taking your life into your own hands. There are plenty of ways to die in a mine shaft, and none of them are pleasant.

The 20-minute drive through the mountainside was both nerve-racking and relaxing. The scenery was calming, but I wanted to get to Alpine Park as soon as possible. With every second that went by, the situation became more dire.

Madison had given me directions to her house, and I had programmed her address into the navigation app on my phone. The route took me through Main Street. It was filled with upscale shopping boutiques, high-end restaurants, bars, hair salons, jewelry stores, and other swanky shops. You could see the slopes, and through the misty air, tiny specks plowed through the snow, skiing down the mountain. High-speed lifts and gondolas carried skiers up to the peak. Several runs already had the lights on for night skiing. This was prime season, and the slopes were packed.

I took Driftwood up the mountain and wound my way through more spires of evergreens and snow-covered banks.

I knew Madison had done well for herself after she sold Diver Down to me, but this was beyond my expectation. I had paid a pretty penny for the restaurant, saving it from the clutches of a developer who would most certainly have knocked it down and turned it into high-rise condos. Her house was a sprawling ski-in ski-out chalet with elegant stonework, large window walls, and a modern but rustic charm.

Low eight figures bought you a cracker box at the base of the mountain a block away from the lift. Hell, covered parking spaces around here went for a cool million. I didn't want to know how much this place cost. Certainly more than what I paid her for Diver Down. But Madison always was quick on her feet. She knew how to turn nothing into something.

An Ice Gray Metallic Macan GTS sat in the driveway.

I parked my rental next to it, climbed out, and moved to the front door. The oak door was tall and majestic, and transom windows above allowed copious amounts of light into the foyer. I rang the video doorbell and waited.

My heart thudded a little. I was nervous. Our last words weren't exactly friendly.

2

Madison pulled open the heavy oak door, and her tortured eyes gazed at me. Without a word, she stepped forward, flung her arms around me, and hugged me tight. "Thanks for coming."

My anxiety about our reunion dissipated, but the situation was still dire.

"Come in," she said.

I stepped into the foyer, pulling my roller case behind me.

She closed the door and looked me up and down. "Well, you look... the same."

I could tell she wasn't entirely impressed with my outfit.

"You haven't aged a day," I said.

It was true. She still had that golden blonde hair, trim figure, and olive skin. But her carefree demeanor was gone. That free spirit had been caged, trapped in a prison of fear. Her blue eyes were a little deeper. Farther away. She had that look a lot of people have after they've been through a major trauma.

This trauma was just beginning.

Madison had once been a model and professional surfer until she blew out her knee. After two ACL reconstructions, she decided to hang up the sport. Seemed like ages ago now.

"Nice place," I said in an understated voice.

"It will do," she teased.

It was nothing short of fantastic.

She led me through the foyer and presented the house.

It was modern yet cozy—5,000 square feet of indoor space, along with 5,000 square feet of outdoor space. Floor-to-ceiling glass offered an impressive connection with nature. Elevated wood plank ceilings, luxurious stonework, and a dramatic fireplace were just some of the highlights. There was a comfortable lounge off the custom kitchen that was fit for a five-star chef. An outdoor dining area with another fireplace and grill and a fire pit with lounge seating was perfect for entertaining. There was a heated, six-car garage, a luxurious spa, a steam room, sauna, another upstairs lounge, and a wrap-around second-story terrace. The guest accommodations and master bedroom were stunning enclaves of peace and serenity. The views were majestic. Fresh powder, frosted evergreens, and snow-capped peaks poked between the clouds.

The sky had turned midnight blue, and glimpses of the waxing moon poked through the clouds.

"They left this," Madison said, handing me a scrap of paper from the butcher block in the kitchen. Her eyes brimmed.

The note was printed from an inkjet and was a collage of different fonts and cut-outs. It read: *You will be contacted with further instructions. Do not call the police. Cooperate, and your daughter and husband will be returned unharmed.*

She had told me over the phone, but reading the note made it all the more real. My stomach twisted. Someone had taken my niece, and though I never met her, it wrecked me just the same. I was determined to get her back safe and sound.

"Have you contacted the authorities?" I asked.

Madison shook her head. "I called you. That's it."

"I want you to run through all the details with me again. When were they taken?"

"I'm not exactly sure. I went out to run some errands this morning. Flynn stayed with Amaryllis."

"Flynn is your husband?"

She nodded. "I think you'd really like him. You'd approve of this one."

Madison hadn't always been the best about picking the right guys. She'd had more than her share of losers. As her older brother, I may have made my opinion known a little too often about some of them. But with Flynn, it seemed like she had found true happiness.

Madison continued. "I have a nanny that comes in to watch Amaryllis from time to time and help out around the house."

"When was the last time she was here?"

"Yesterday. She works at my restaurant. It's really great because I can adjust her schedule, and she's available when I need her. Tara's a really sweet girl."

"You have another restaurant?"

She nodded. "We just opened a month ago."

"Have you told Tara?"

Madison shook her head again. "I haven't told anyone but you."

I picked up where she left off. "So, you went into town, ran some errands, and came back..."

"It was a little after 11:00 AM when I found the note. I called you right away."

"Have you heard anything from the kidnappers?"

"No," she said, biting her bottom lip. Worry tensed her brow.

"Do you have any security cameras?"

She shook her head. "Just the video doorbell."

"Pull up the footage from that time."

"I looked. There's nothing unusual."

"Who else has access to the property?"

"Just me and Flynn. Tara has a key."

"You're on the mountain. Anyone could ski up to the house." I paused. "What about maintenance people, contractors, etc.?"

"We just moved in a month ago. We're still getting settled. We were in a rental a few months before that until we could get in. We sold our place in Denver."

"You have a picture of Amaryllis handy?"

Madison nodded.

She pulled her phone from a pocket, launched the photos app, and thumbed through a few pictures. She showed me an image of an adorable young girl. "She just turned three."

I stared at the photo in disbelief. Had it been that long? It seemed like yesterday when Madison left Coconut Key.

Amaryllis had the same golden blonde hair, blue eyes, and enchanting features. There was no mistaking her as Madison's child.

"What about Flynn?"

Madison took the phone back, swiped to another set of images, then handed the device back to me. Flynn was a handsome man in his early 40s with rugged good looks, ice-blue eyes, shaggy brown hair, and a trimmed beard.

"You know if he left the house while you were gone?"

"He didn't tell me he was going anywhere. He would have called me to let me know."

"Were there any signs of forced entry?"

Madison shook her head again. "No. But we really don't lock our doors."

I stared at her in disbelief.

"What!?" she said with a shrug. "It's a small town. There are few break-ins."

"I worked a murder case here last year," I said. "This town isn't quite as angelic as some might believe."

"We've been coming here for the last few years to ski. Flynn and I both wanted to get out of Denver. This house became available, and we jumped at the opportunity."

"So, you bought a new house and a new restaurant?"

Madison nodded. "Flynn and I figured we could manage it together. Lord knows I've got the experience. How is Diver Down, by the way?"

"Great."

"Still the same?"

"We upgraded the marina, added a few menu items, but I'm never changing that place."

"Never say never."

"What does Flynn do for a living?"

"Like I said, he's managing the restaurant with me. Before that, he was in IT."

"Looks like you've done well for yourself."

"I made some smart moves. Turned what I had into a lot more. This was supposed to be our semi-retirement."

"You call running a restaurant retirement?"

"It's just something I wanted to do. I can be a mom and still have a career. It's not like we are depending on it."

"Who's got more money? You or Flynn?"

"What does that matter?"

I shrugged.

"Flynn didn't marry me for my money, if that's what you're getting at. He didn't know how much I had until after we got together. Do you know how hard it is to find a good guy these days? Sure, there are plenty of rich guys around here, but all they want are playthings. Hot, young, and dumb."

"How's your relationship with Flynn?"

Her brow knitted with annoyance. "Great. Why?"

I shrugged ominously. "He was looking after Amaryllis. He disappears with her. He wouldn't be the first dad to run off with his kid."

Madison looked mortified. "That's ridiculous!"

"I'm just keeping my mind open to the possibilities. And you should too."

"That's not a possibility, okay? Flynn and I have a wonderful relationship. He's the kindest, most caring man I've ever met. And he loves his daughter. He's a good dad. Don't start."

I raised my hands in surrender. I'd struck a nerve. "You asked for my help. I'm here for you. I just want to be thorough."

She nodded and softened. "I understand."

"Have you tried calling him?"

"Of course. He didn't pick up." She paused. "You have ways to track cell phones, don't you?"

I nodded.

I had called Isabella the minute Madison informed me of the situation. Isabella was my handler at Cobra Company. The off-the-books clandestine agency had immense resources. She could find out just about anything about anyone. Her methods weren't always legal, and none of the intel she acquired could be used in a court of law unless we had gotten a prior warrant.

"The last time his phone pinged a cell tower was this morning at this location," I said.

"What does that mean?"

"Cell phones connect with the tower at regular intervals and any time you use the network."

"I know that. I mean, what does it tell you?"

"It tells me the kidnappers were smart enough to turn off Flynn's device before they left the premises. From the data, they were also smart enough not to carry devices connected to a cellular network. No other phones pinged the tower from this location except for yours."

I walked around the house, looking for any signs of forced entry. There were no broken windows. No sign that any locks had been tampered with.

The doors were locked now.

"How private are you about your wealth?" I asked.

"I'm not flaunting it all over the Internet, if that's what you mean. I have social media accounts like everybody else, but I'm not posting pictures of expensive clothing, lavish vacations, or expensive cars."

"You buy a house like this, you become a target. This place wasn't cheap."

"No, it wasn't."

"How well-off is Flynn?"

"He made a comfortable living."

"But not your kind of wealth."

"No."

"After the sale of Diver Down, you had a pretty good starting point."

"Still bitter about that, are you?"

I smiled. "Nope. Not at all."

"It's probably worth double what you paid for it."

"In this market, it probably is."

There was a long silence between us.

"I need you to be straight with me," Madison said in a grave tone. "I know you deal with this type of thing a lot. What are the odds of getting them both back alive?"

3

"**I**'m going to do everything I can to get them back," I said.

Madison gave a solemn nod.

"I'm not going to pull any punches. These are delicate situations. We don't know what type of people we're dealing with yet." I paused. "Are you at odds with anybody right now? Anybody with a vendetta?"

She hesitated a moment. "Well, I've been having a little trouble with Simon Holt."

I lifted a curious brow. "You've only been in town a couple months, and you've already got trouble?"

She gave me a sassy look. "You can stir up trouble a whole hell of a lot faster than that."

I couldn't argue.

"He owned the restaurant before I did. The bank foreclosed on it. I bought it, renovated it, and he approached me a few weeks ago to buy it back. I'm not selling. He tossed out a generous offer, but I wasn't interested. It's not about the money for me." She paused. "Came by the house once. He was nice but persistent. I understand he went through some hardship, but... I told him I'd let him know if I ever wanted to sell. Then last week, the restaurant was vandalized. Windows were broken out. I think that was a message."

"Did you report it?"

"Of course. A deputy came out, and I made an official report. Haven't heard anything since."

"Sounds like an intimidation tactic," I said. "Got a beef with anybody else?"

"Not that I can think of."

"What about Flynn? Does he have any enemies?"

She thought about it for a moment. "Not that I know of."

"Have you noticed anyone unusual around the property?"

Madison thought about it for a moment. "There was a drifter that came by a few days ago, looking for work. He rang the bell. I didn't recognize him. I just talked to him through the speaker."

"Can you show me the clip?"

Madison nodded and thumbed through her phone again. She scrolled through the timeline on the video doorbell and replayed the clip for me. The guy was tall and skinny, in his late 20s, early 30s. He had shaggy, golden brown hair, a scruffy beard, and a backpack slung over his shoulder. It was a little cold out to be drifting around these parts, but there were inventive ways to stay warm in the wintertime, and there was a homeless shelter in town that provided a warm bunk and a hot meal. Alpine Park wasn't the kind of place that had a big homeless population, but there were those that preferred to live *close to nature*, let's just say.

She exported the clip and sent it to my phone.

I sent a text message to Isabella and asked her to pull background on Flynn Foster and Tara Preston. Despite what Madison said, my suspicious nature forced me to investigate all possibilities. I sent the image of the drifter as well. Isabella might be able to get a hit on facial recognition. I asked her to monitor Madison's incoming calls. The kidnappers would have to get in contact at some point in time.

"What do we do now?" Madison asked.

"We wait," I said. "I have a contact at the local sheriff's office. We can contact the FBI. They will assist when requested, even though this isn't a federal case yet."

"They said no cops."

"I'll call my contact. She'll be discreet about it. We can choose whether or not to bring in the feds, if need be."

"What are the pros and cons?"

"More resources. On the downside, it could agitate them. They may retaliate. Though, that seems unlikely. If they damage the merchandise, they're not getting the ransom."

Madison cringed at the thought. "I have a low-risk tolerance."

"I understand."

"My priority is that I get my daughter and my husband back. They can have all of my money. I don't care. There is nothing more valuable to me."

I nodded in agreement.

She exhaled some of the tension. "It's good to see you. I wish it were under different circumstances."

"Me too." I paused. "I'll need to speak with Tara."

"I'll give her a call."

Just as Madison was about to dial, her phone buzzed with an unknown number. Panic filled her eyes as she stared at the display for a moment. "Do you think this is them?"

4

"Hello?" Madison eked out in a timid voice.

I whispered in her ear to put the call on speaker.

She did.

A garbled, distorted voice crackled through the line. The kind of voice that made your skin crawl. "We have Flynn and Amaryllis. If you want to see them alive, you'll do exactly as we say."

"What do you want?"

"$10 million. We've done our research, and we know that's well within your capabilities."

"I want my daughter and my husband back right now!" Madison demanded.

"You are not in charge. You will be given instructions on where to transfer the money."

"Get proof of life," I whispered.

Madison looked confused, but my expression urged her on.

"I need proof of life," she stammered. "I want to talk to my daughter."

"Get a video," I whispered in her ear.

"I want video proof as well."

"Who's with you?"

"Nobody."

"Lie to me again, and your daughter will die."

"If any harm comes to either of them, you'll never see a dime from me," Madison said, growing bold. "And money will be the least of your worries."

There was a long pause.

Static crackled through the line.

"Who's with you?"

Madison hesitated. "My brother."

I motioned for Madison to give me the phone. She handed it over. I wanted to tear into the guy and tell him how painful I was going to make his death. But I put on my negotiator hat, bit my tongue, and smiled. "Hey, I'm Tyson," I said in a soothing voice. "Who am I talking to?"

"It's none of your business. All you need to know is that we mean what we say."

"Sounds like you got yourself into a difficult situation."

"How do you figure?"

"You've got two hostages. One of them is going to be more difficult to care for than the other. The stakes are high, and things could end up badly for you. But if you let me help you out, we can come to the best resolution for everyone involved."

"The best resolution would be for you to hand over the $10 million and get your loved ones back."

"How about this... You let Amaryllis and Flynn go, and I'll forget all about this little incident. We'll chalk it up to a misunderstanding."

"There seems to be something missing from that equation."

"I'm trying to stop you from making a terrible mistake. Because I don't think you're fully aware of the repercussions of your actions."

"There won't be any repercussions."

"I can assure you, there will be if any harm comes to either of them."

"Do as you're told, and everyone will get what they want."

"Just so we're clear, I will hunt down and kill every last one of you involved. It doesn't matter where you go or how long it takes."

There was a momentary pause.

"I'm not sure you're in a position to make threats. I can make threats of my own."

"If you harm them, you get nothing."

"Right now, they are in excellent condition. Keep antagonizing me, and we might have a scratch and dent sale."

My jaw clenched tight, and rage boiled.

"This conversation is over."

The line went dead, and Madison glared at me. "What the hell was that?"

"Just laying out the facts for them."

"Newsflash, this may be a game to you. But this is my family."

"This is no game. I meant every word I said. I will track them down and break a few personal rules."

"None of that matters if Amaryllis or Flynn are dead."

"At this point, we don't even know if they have them. Until we get confirmation, we have to work under the assumption that..." A grim look flashed on my face.

Madison read my expression loud and clear. "Don't say it. Don't you dare say it."

I kept my mouth shut, but there was a real possibility that they were already dead.

I called Isabella. "Were you able to track that incoming call?"

5

"Sorry, I wasn't able to track the call," Isabella said. "Seems like they know what they're doing, to some degree. They bounced the call through an encrypted network and multiple proxy servers."

"I figured that was the case."

"As for Tara and Flynn. They're both clean. Nothing stands out in their background. I'll keep digging and let you know if I find anything."

"What about the drifter?"

"Face recognition got a match. Guy's name is Wyatt Kendall. Multiple arrests for trespassing, vagrancy, public intoxication—typical charges that go along with living on the street. Nothing violent. But there's a first time for everything."

I thanked her for the information and ended the call, then dialed Dakota Skye. It had been a while since I'd spoken to her.

She answered in a cheery but snarky tone. "Now there's a number that hasn't graced my phone in quite a while. To what do I owe the pleasure?"

"Deputy Skye, so nice to hear your voice."

"It's not deputy anymore. It's Sheriff Skye to you, Mister."

"Impressive. I always knew you had it in you."

"Yeah, well, the town didn't have much choice after what happened to Bosco Dean."

"I'm sure Alpine Park is much better off."

She chuckled. "Possibly. What can I do for you?"

"It seems fate has brought me back into town."

"Oh, really?"

"I need a favor."

"Sounds serious."

"It is."

I gave her the details.

Dakota gasped. "That's horrible! What can I do?"

"Keep this between us for the time being. I'm sure your department is trustworthy. But they didn't want any authorities involved."

"You're involved."

"I'm not really an authority in this jurisdiction."

"Never stopped you before," she muttered. "As you're aware, this is out of our area. We rarely deal with this kind of thing."

"I know."

"But my department is at your disposal," she said.

"I appreciate that."

"You want me to call the FBI?"

"Not yet."

"I know you have resources far beyond what we have here, but..."

"Your support means everything. It's nice to not butt heads with the local sheriff for a change."

"Where are you? I can be there in a few minutes."

"I'm with my sister, Madison Foster."

"Your sister is Madison Foster? Small world."

"It feels that way at times."

"She bought the old Pine residence. I can see why she became a target." Dakota paused. "You think they're watching the house?"

"Could be. I think we should assume they are keeping a close eye on the situation. I would."

"I'll take my personal vehicle and be there in a few minutes."

"I'd appreciate that. It will be good to see you."

Her voice softened a bit. "You too, Deputy."

I ended the call and slid the phone back into my pocket.

Dakota Skye and I had quite an adventure together last winter.

"Old girlfriend?" Madison asked, having listened intently to the conversation.

"Girlfriend might be a strong term."

Madison rolled her eyes. "So you shagged the local sheriff?"

"She wasn't the sheriff then."

"Well, if she helps get my family back, she'll be my new best friend."

Madison called Tara and told her to come to the house. She urged her to be quiet about the situation.

Dakota arrived in a red Wrangler several minutes later. She had ditched her duty jacket and wore a powder jacket, but she still looked like a cop. The swagger is hard to hide. She rang the bell, and I answered the door. Dakota flashed a grim smile when she saw me and gave me a hug. "Good to see you."

"Likewise," I said. "Thanks for coming."

"Absolutely."

We broke from our awkward embrace just as Madison entered the foyer.

"Have you two met?" I asked.

"Not formally," Dakota said.

She extended her hand. The two shook and exchanged pleasantries.

"I'm sorry about your situation," Dakota said.

A sparkling engagement ring on Dakota's finger caught the light. Maybe that's why we fell out of touch.

"Rest assured, you will have my department's full support," Dakota said. "And I don't need to tell you this, but you couldn't have a better person on the case than your brother."

Madison forced a tight smile and looked at me with appreciative eyes.

A few minutes later, a silver GLA Mercedes pulled up. A gorgeous young brunette hopped out and jogged to the door. She knocked lightly, then stepped inside. She rushed to embrace Madison. "Oh my God, are you okay?"

Madison nodded and introduced us. I figured it was Tara. She was 19 with long raven hair, ice-blue eyes, and features that were easy to look at—full lips, sculpted cheekbones, and smooth, creamy skin. She looked like the face of a teen makeup brand.

Tara nodded at the sheriff.

"I have a few questions for you," I said.

"Sure," Tara replied. "Do you have any idea who's responsible?"

"That's what we're trying to figure out."

"Have they made demands yet?"

I nodded.

"You can just pay them and get Amaryllis and Flynn back, right?"

"It's not always that easy," I said. "Have you noticed anyone suspicious around the property lately? Any strange phone calls here at the house?"

Tara shook her head. She thought about it for a moment, then added, "Oh, wait a minute. There was this guy who came by the other day. I don't know if this is important or not. Said he used to live here, and that he left something inside. He said the property was sold before he had a chance to get it."

"You didn't tell me about this," Madison said, concern tensing her brow.

Tara cringed. "I'm sorry. I forgot. I meant to tell you. I told him he'd have to come back later and ask you. I thought it was bullshit." She cringed again. "Excuse my language. You know, these freaks will say anything to get inside, then they'll do God knows what."

"Did he say his name?" I asked.

"Said his name was Quentin Pine."

That piqued Dakota's interest. "When was this?"

"About a week ago, maybe," Tara said.

I told Madison to look through the video feed from the doorbell. She scrolled back a week and found the interaction. We all huddled over the device and studied the clip.

"It looks like Quentin, alright," Dakota said. She pulled me aside and muttered, "He just got out of state prison."

I lifted an intrigued brow.

"His father owned the place before Madison. Quentin did a nickel for B&E."

"The guy's breaking into homes while his dad lived in a place like this?"

"Quentin has been in trouble with the law around here for as long as I can remember. Possession, DUI, drunk and disorderly. That kind of thing. He went down a bad path, got into drugs, and that's when he started knocking off houses. His dad disowned him. I heard he was cut out of the will."

"What do you think he was after?"

Dakota shrugged.

"There was nothing in the house when we moved in," Madison said. "Everything was gone. I don't know what he could possibly want."

"Maybe he just wanted to get inside," I said. "Maybe he was casing the place."

"Kidnapping seems like a step up for him," Dakota said. "Especially after he just got out. You'd think after doing a little hard time, you wouldn't want to go back to prison."

"Sometimes people go to prison and pick up new skills. Other people become institutionalized. They grow accustomed to the life. They feel naked on the outside, and subconsciously, they want to go back in."

"Okay, *Mr. Psychology*."

I shrugged. "You know where we can find him?"

"The state has a mandatory parole for certain offenses. B&E is a Class 3 felony. Quentin will be under supervision for five years. He'll have to maintain a record of his whereabouts with the state."

"I say we pay him a visit. Also, we need to look into a drifter named Wyatt Kendall."

"In this weather, he shouldn't be hard to find."

"The shelter?"

Dakota nodded.

"Let's get on this," I said.

I asked Madison if she would be okay while I was gone. Tara agreed to stay with her and keep her company.

"Do you have a gun in the house?" I asked.

Madison shook her head.

"I'm going to give you one."

"I don't need a gun."

"After what happened, yes, you do."

I dug into my bag and gave her a small subcompact that I carried as a backup. "I know you know how to use this." She nodded. "Just remember that I'm staying with you, and don't shoot me when I come back."

"I've got an extra key for you," she said.

"And make sure all the doors are locked," I cautioned.

She and Tara both nodded.

Madison hustled into the kitchen, rummaged through a drawer, and returned a moment later with a spare key. She gave it to me, and I slipped it onto my key ring. "You call me if you need anything."

"I will."

"You sure you're going to be okay?"

Madison nodded.

Dakota and I stepped outside and hurried to her vehicle. I climbed into the passenger seat, and she slid behind the wheel. Dakota cranked up the engine, put the car into gear, and backed up. She spun around and headed down the driveway to Red Fox Ridge, then meandered toward Driftwood.

"I'm gone a year, and a lot changes," I said.

Dakota gave me a look. She knew what I was getting at.

"What do you think about Tara?"

"She's a good girl," Dakota said. "Stays out of trouble. Her brother gets into it every now and then, but nothing too terrible. A few speeding tickets and a DUI. He got picked up on a controlled substance charge. Later dismissed. But around here, throw a stick and you'll hit someone with a gram of coke in their pocket."

"What about Flynn?"

"Don't really know the guy. They both just came to town. Hell, I didn't know she was your sister until you told me."

"What's it like being the new sheriff?"

Dakota grinned. "Well, as they say, the buck stops here. I'm the one everybody blames when everything goes to hell."

"I'm sure you run a tight ship."

"As tight as can be. It's more politics than anything else. I've got the mayor and city council up my ass on a regular basis. Honestly, I think I liked being a deputy better."

"I'm sure you make a good sheriff."

"Didn't have much of a choice."

"Are you gonna run for re-election?"

"I've got a little time to think about that."

"I don't think Alpine Park can do better," I said.

She gave me a look.

"What? It's true!"

"Anybody is better than Bosco Dean. But getting rid of him hasn't really solved our problem. It just opened a door for somebody else to step in. This town still has the same old problems, and changing sheriffs didn't make that go away."

I frowned. "Not surprising."

Sometimes, as a cop, you felt like you were just pulling weeds. The minute you got a nasty one out of the ground, another one sprang up.

"I see that's not the only thing that changed around here," I added.

She knew what I was getting at and wiggled her ring finger as she gripped the steering wheel. "What was I going to do? Wait around for you forever?" She scoffed.

I laughed.

We both knew it wasn't that serious between us.

"We had a moment, and I enjoyed that moment," she said.

"I'm happy for you, if you're happy."

She smiled. "I am happy."

"Whoever he is, he's a lucky man."

She grinned. "Yes. Yes, he is."

"He'd better know it."

"If he doesn't, I'll kick his ass."

I chuckled again.

Dakota's headlights illuminated the roadway as we weaved our way down Driftwood back toward town. The evergreens blurred by.

"Can you think of anybody who might be responsible for something like this?"

Dakota sighed. "Alpine Park is one of the richest areas in the country. If you're going to target someone for kidnapping and ransom, this is the place to do it. Honestly, I'm surprised we haven't seen more of this kind of thing. People think they're in a bubble here. It's a playground. They walk around completely oblivious to the dangers."

We drove into town and made our way to the Alpine Mission. Dakota found a place to park, and we hopped out. She traded her powder jacket for her duty coat and stepped back into the role of sheriff.

With the sun beyond the horizon, it got cold, fast.

Dakota sized me up as we strolled the sidewalk to the entrance of the shelter. She snarked, "I see you're taking casual to a new level."

"It's a long story. I'll tell you about it sometime."

6

It was probably the most expensive homeless shelter in the country. The property value was astronomical. Still, it was a far cry from the ski-in, ski-out chalets on the mountain or the sprawling countryside estates. But it was warm and protected from the elements. The air smelled like a mix of stew and baked bread, mixed with the scent of stale coffee, dirty clothes, and the lack of deodorant.

The motivational posters on the wall weren't inspiring anyone. The optimistic slogans were largely ignored.

Rows and rows of bunks lined the sleeping quarters. Unlike most gymnasium-type shelters, there were no harsh over-head fluorescents. Each bunk had a small dresser with lock-able drawers. Lamps were hardwired into the main switch. It was lights out at 10:00 PM. Despite the constant traffic, the staff kept the place meticulously clean—you had to be in a place like this. The last thing anyone wanted was some type of outbreak.

Painted in earth tones, the place was about as cozy as you could get for this type of shelter. For some, there was no incentive to leave. There was a dining area and a library full of hardbacks and paperbacks that had been donated—the pages yellowed with age and the covers worn.

Few ventured into the area.

Soothing background music played through the speakers, and the subtle murmur of conversation drifted about. Some tried to sleep early, others were lost in their own thoughts, in their own world.

Dakota and I scanned the lonely faces, looking for the drifter. We spotted Wyatt in the dining hall. He'd just dished up a plate. Dakota saw him first and pointed him out.

Wyatt noticed. He stiffened, and panic filled his eyes.

A lot of people have that reaction when a cop points at them.

Wyatt dropped the plate, and the food splattered. The utensils clattered against the floor. He sprinted for the back exit, and we chased after him, weaving through the crowd, trying not to topple more plates. We weren't always successful, and that drew more than a few angry growls.

Wyatt burst through the exit into the sharp cold.

We followed and chased him down a back alley. Snow flurries drifted through the air, and my heavy breath fogged.

Wyatt rounded a corner at the end of the alley, and I darted after him at full speed. I hit a patch of ice and busted my ass on the concrete.

Wyatt darted across the street amid traffic. Horns honked, and cars swerved. He flickered through the headlight beams and disappeared into another alley, long gone.

"You're not in Florida anymore," Dakota said with a smirk as she caught up to me.

"Thanks for the heads up. I hadn't noticed."

She chuckled, gave me a hand, and helped me off the ground.

My elbow throbbed, but I'd survive. "Any idea where he'd go?"

"No, but I'll put a BOLO out on him. He'll turn up." Dakota paused. "Something tells me if he was involved in a kidnapping, he wouldn't be hanging around a homeless shelter."

"You're probably right about that. But why did he run?"

"Because he's probably holding something he doesn't want us to find. Maybe he's done something else he's guilty of. Petty theft. Who knows?"

We headed back to Dakota's Wrangler and climbed in. She cranked up the engine and blasted the heat. "Where to?"

"Know where we can find Simon Holt?"

She nodded. I told her about the vandalism of the restaurant. "Is he the type to do something like that?"

"He was pretty desperate for a while," Dakota said. "That restaurant had been in his family forever. He got himself in a pinch cash-wise and couldn't make the numbers work. Lost the restaurant. Lost his house. Went through some tough times. I feel bad for the guy. His wife passed. His world really fell apart. Somehow, he managed to turn things around and get most of it back, except for the restaurant. He seems dead set on reacquiring it."

7

Simon Holt lived in a condo at the base of the mountain, not far from the lift. Dakota put a fist against his fourth-floor door.

Footsteps shuffled down the foyer, and Simon answered a moment later.

He was in his early 50s with a friendly face and dark brown hair with hints of gray. His hairline was receding at the corners and thinning at the peak. He had a healthy tan from the slopes, which was lighter around the eyes from the sunglasses. It was a common look around the resort.

He looked at us with curiosity. "Deputy Skye, what can I do for you?"

"It's Sheriff Skye."

"Of course. Old habits."

"We just have a few questions."

He put on a good face but tensed a little.

"The Silverado was vandalized last week," Dakota said.

"I heard. Such a shame. This town is really going downhill." It was a not-so-subtle jab. I don't think he was a fan of Dakota's department.

"It's my understanding that you're looking to reacquire the restaurant."

"I am. The owner seems to be reluctant to sell, even though I made quite a nice offer."

"She just purchased it."

"I'm offering a considerable amount more than she paid for it. I would call that an opportunity. A fast way to get a return on your investment."

"Why not start a new restaurant in a new location?" I asked.

"Because I want *that* restaurant at *that* location. And in case you hadn't noticed, real estate is tight around here. Besides, the business has sentimental value. Is it a crime to want your property back?"

"No, but vandalism is, among other things."

His eyes narrowed at Sheriff Skye. "What are you suggesting?"

"It's my understanding that you've been harassing Mrs. Foster on a regular basis about selling. I'm just curious about how far you're willing to go to get your property back."

His jaw tightened, and his eyes blazed into her. "I don't appreciate you showing up at my door, making wild accusations."

"I'm not making any accusations. I'm just asking questions."

"You're insinuating that I had some involvement in the vandalism, that I've been harassing and pressuring Mrs. Foster to sell. Neither of those is true. I've merely made my wishes known. If she ever decides to sell the restaurant, she knows where to find a buyer."

"Have you ever visited Mrs. Foster at home?"

"Once. I thought I'd stop by and introduce myself. Put a face to a name. Apparently, my charm wasn't enough."

"When was the last time you were at her property?"

"Two weeks ago. I brought her a housewarming gift. Is that illegal too?"

"What did you bring her?"

"A bottle of wine. A very nice bottle of wine. Expensive."

"If you don't mind my asking, how did you lose the restaurant in the first place?" I said.

Simon looked at me with annoyed eyes. "My wife fell ill. That took time and attention away from the business. The restaurant declined. I had expenses related to her medical care at the same time that I was trying to expand and upgrade the property. Combined with a few bad financial moves, I got into a bind. Sadly, my wife passed. I'm trying to put my life back together one piece at a time."

"I'm sorry for your loss," I said.

"Can you tell me where you've been all day?" Dakota asked.

Isabella had tracked his phone. The device had been at the condo all day. If I were going to engage in criminal activity,

I'd leave my phone at home to establish somewhat of an alibi.

His face wrinkled with offense. "Why?"

"There's been some criminal activity at the Foster residence."

"What kind of criminal activity?"

"I can't discuss that at the moment."

"And you think I had some type of involvement?"

"It's a serious matter, and we're interviewing everyone who was at odds with Mrs. Foster."

"I'm not at odds with Mrs. Foster. I'm sure she's a nice woman."

"You mind if we take a look around your apartment?"

His face crinkled again. "You want to do what!? No! Absolutely not." He glared at us for a moment, his cheeks flushed. "Now, if you'll excuse me, Sheriff, I've had my fill of your questions."

He closed the door and latched the deadbolt.

Dakota and I exchanged a look.

"Well, if I do run for re-election, he's not going to vote for me," she said dryly.

We left the building and headed back to her vehicle.

"You know Simon better than I do. What are your thoughts?"

Dakota shrugged. "The guy has been through a lot. But what's the play? Kidnap Amaryllis and Flynn to force Madison to sell? To scare her off? Seems extreme."

I agreed. Simon wasn't high on my list, but I didn't have much to go on.

We climbed into the Wrangler, and Dakota made a phone call. "Hey babe, I'm going to be running a little late. Some things came up."

I couldn't help but overhear the conversation.

"Things always come up," the voice groaned.

"This is pretty serious stuff," Dakota said.

"When do you think you'll stop by?"

"You know the drill."

"I do."

"We'll have to do dinner another night. I'll call you when I'm on my way to my apartment. If it's not too late, I might stop by. Love you."

"Love you, too."

She ended the call and started the engine.

"It's tough, isn't it?" I said.

"He wants me around more. But that's not a bad thing."

We left Alpine Park and drove down the mountain. Quentin Pine lived in the neighboring town of Cedar Springs with his girlfriend. At least, that's the information that was given to his parole officer.

8

For the price of an exotic Italian sports car, you could get a luxurious, single-wide trailer in Cedar Springs. A 1,000-square-foot, two-bedroom, two-bath *estate*. No lawn to maintain, just a gravel drive in front of the house.

We pulled up to the forest green home at 14 Shady Glen. It had white trim and a small addition built onto the side. Two evergreens stood guard.

The neighborhood was well maintained, nestled at the base of the mountain, just off the highway. A lot of people that worked in Alpine Park lived in Cedar Springs. If you loved to ski and the outdoors, it wasn't a bad option. Relatively affordable, given the area.

There were a few lights on inside and a maroon Toyota sedan in the driveway.

We hopped out, crunched across the snowy gravel, and climbed the steps. Dakota banged on the front door.

Footsteps shuffled, and a moment later, a woman in her mid-30s answered.

"Are you Deborah Wilks?" Dakota asked.

Concern filled her eyes as she nodded. "Yes. Is there some kind of problem?"

She was a pear-shaped woman with curly brown hair that hung to her shoulders, tawny eyes, a round face, and a double chin.

"No problem," Sheriff Skye assured. "Is Quentin around?"

"No. Why? He's not in some kind of trouble, is he?" She said it like she expected trouble with Quentin.

"No ma'am. We just have a few routine questions for him. He lives here with you, yes?"

She nodded.

"You know where he is right now?"

"I don't know. I haven't heard from him all day." Her tone was irritated.

"Is he currently employed?"

"He works for a friend, doing construction. Odd jobs, remodeling. That kind of thing."

"Was he working today?" I asked.

"I suppose. He left in the morning."

"How did you two meet?" I asked.

She squinted at me. "What business is that of yours?"

"Just curious."

"I had known Quentin before. We started talking again when he was in prison." She looked away, embarrassed. "I know that seems crazy. But Quentin can be really sweet when he wants to be."

By her demeanor, I got the impression that it wasn't all roses and sunshine since Quentin's release.

"Is he staying on the straight and narrow?"

"I'll kick his ass outta here if he's not." Her voice grew stern. "I will not tolerate any drug use in my home."

"Is he drinking?"

"You'd have to ask him," she said, knowing damn good and well what his proclivities were. "He hasn't done something to violate his parole, has he?"

"Has he talked to you about any... illegal activities?"

Her face tensed again. "What's he gotten himself into?"

"I'm not sure." I hesitated. "We're investigating a kidnapping."

Deborah's eyes rounded. "A kidnapping?"

"We're looking into people who may have a connection."

"A connection?"

"Quentin stopped by his father's old residence the other day," Dakota said. "You know what he may have been after?"

"No." She hesitated. "I'd call him, but he ran off without his phone. He does that sometimes. I think he'd forget his head if it wasn't screwed on. Then again, maybe he does it on purpose."

"Do you have his employer's number handy?" I asked.

"Believe me, I called Rick, but he hasn't returned my call." She paused, and her eyes narrowed. "You don't really think Quentin's involved in some type of kidnapping, do you?"

"We're just looking at all the felons in the area," I said.

"When you put it like that, it sounds bad. Convicted felon." Deborah frowned and shook her head. "My mother would be proud." She facepalmed. "I just get so lonely."

Her voice cracked, and tears brimmed.

"It's okay," Dakota assured.

Deborah sniffled, and tears streamed. After a moment, she pulled herself together. "I'll get you Rick's number."

"Do you mind if we look around the property?" I asked.

Deborah hesitated. "Uh, sure. Go ahead."

She stepped aside, and we entered the home.

"This is serious, isn't it?" she asked in a grave tone.

"Kidnappings typically are," Dakota replied.

"If he's involved in something like that, he's not getting back in this house," she declared, her eyes still red, her nose runny. "I can assure you of that."

The interior was about as nice as a single wide could be. It had gray vinyl flooring that simulated hardwoods, a living area with cozy furniture, a kitchen with laminate counter-tops, and a hallway that led to the bedrooms. It was tidy, and the kitchen was clean.

Deborah grabbed her phone, and Dakota gave her a business card. She texted Rick's information.

There wasn't much to search, and I didn't find anything unusual.

Dakota stayed with Deborah while I stepped outside and checked the small shed. Neither Amaryllis nor Flynn were being held captive here. That was certain.

I returned inside and said to Deborah, "I'd appreciate it if you kept our visit between us. This is a delicate matter."

She nodded. "Quentin's never done anything violent." She sighed. "I know, I know. He broke into a few homes. *Allegedly*. But he's just not the violent sort."

"I hope that's the case," Dakota said. "If you hear from him, give me a call. Anytime, day or night."

We left the house and walked back to the Wrangler.

"We need to find Quentin ASAP," Dakota said as she slipped behind the wheel. "He's our best lead yet."

"He conveniently left his phone at home today," I said in a suspicious tone.

Dakota forwarded Rick's number to me. I dialed, but there was no answer.

Then I dialed Isabella. My suspicion intensified when she told me Rick's phone was off the grid as well.

9

We drove back to Alpine Park. I was lost in thought on the way, the drone of the highway filling the vehicle. Sparse headlights passed occasionally. Otherwise, the road was dark and empty. Cloud cover obscured the moon as we drove the winding road through the mountains, past the endless expanse of evergreens.

Dakota's phone buzzed again. She answered in a soft voice. This was a personal call. "I'm heading back now."

"Okay, just checking in on you."

"I'm gonna drop a friend off, then I'll be there shortly."

"A friend?"

"A colleague," she said in a hushed tone. "We'll talk later."

She ended the call and slipped the phone back into her pocket.

I tried to bite my tongue, but I had to say something. "He's a little..."

"Overprotective?"

"You said it, not me."

She smiled. "Wouldn't you want to protect what's valuable to you?"

"Absolutely."

I hesitated, then said, "I'm sure he's a great guy. I'd love to meet him sometime."

Dakota balked. "Oh, no! You two are never meeting. I'm of the mind that he doesn't need to see us together. I don't want to know about his former life, and he does not need to have mine rubbed in his face. He doesn't need anything to add to his insecurity."

"So, he's insecure," I said flatly.

"Not insecure." She chose her words. "It's just that not everybody can live up to your..."

"My what?" I said, trying to stifle a grin.

"Energy, for lack of a better word."

"Energy?" I said, amused.

"Tyson, I'm not going to stroke your ego, but you have certain... desirable characteristics."

I tried not to smile, but it was growing more difficult. "And what characteristics would those be?"

"Like I said, I don't need to inflate your ego any more than it already is."

"I don't have a big ego," I said innocently.

She gave me a look and blushed a little. "This conversation is over."

I chuckled.

We made it back to Alpine Park, and she drove me up Driftwood to Red Fox Ridge and dropped me off at Madison's estate. She parked in front of the house, the engine idling. It was an awkward moment.

"Listen, I really appreciate your support," I said.

"It's my job. And it's what friends do."

We stared at each other for a moment.

"Keep me posted," she said.

I nodded and climbed out of the vehicle.

Dakota drove away, and I ambled inside. I found Madison and Tara in the living room. The television was on, but Madison was lost in her own world.

"Did you find anything?" she asked, snapping out of her trance as I entered.

"Some possible leads, but nothing really." I gave her a recap of the evening. "Have you received proof of life?"

A grim frown tensed her face as she shook her head. Her eyes teared up. "What if she's...?"

She stood up and gave me a sad embrace.

"Don't go there. I'm sure they're both fine."

"Is it usual for them to delay sending proof of life for this long?"

"There is nothing standard about any of this. But, typically, kidnappers want you to know that they have the merchandise and it is in good condition."

"Madison, if you don't mind, it's getting late," Tara said. "I'm going to go home."

"Sure thing, Sweetie. It was so kind of you to stay with me."

"I'm here for you."

Tara gave Madison a hug, and the two girls teared up.

"It's going to be okay," Tara assured. "I know it is."

Madison nodded.

Tara said goodbye and snuck out.

I told Madison to get some rest.

"Are you kidding me? I can't sleep. I'm a nervous wreck."

"I'm not encouraging anything, but... if you have anything that might help you relax..."

"I'm not a big smoker, but Flynn has some weed around here. It's legal," she reminded me with big eyes.

"I know."

"It might just settle my nerves a little."

I raised my hands innocently.

"Let me show you to your room."

She escorted me up to the second floor. The guest bedroom was elegant. It had its own balcony that looked out over the slopes. The tile was heated in the bathroom, and it had a flatscreen display, a queen-size bed, and a few comfy chairs. The room had light carpet and stone walls, offset by wood plank ceilings and wood paneling against the headboard.

"I'm just down the hall," Madison said. "My house is your house. Help yourself to anything in the fridge."

"I'm going to walk the perimeter and make sure things are locked up. If you need me, just shout. And announce yourself. You're not the only one on edge."

She nodded before leaving. Madison ambled down the hall to the master bedroom, slipped inside, and closed the door.

After securing the premises, I grabbed my bag, found my overnight kit, and brushed my teeth. I settled in for bed and tried to unwind. Like Madison, there was no way I could get restful sleep—not with Amaryllis and Flynn out there in captivity.

My phone buzzed with a text from JD a little after 1:00 AM —2:00 AM Texas time. [*How's it going? Show went great. I'll be up there in the morning. Catching the red eye.*]

I filled him in on the details, then figured I should at least try to get some sleep. Something told me it would be a tense few days with little downtime.

I didn't know then how right I was.

I had dozed off by 2:00 AM Colorado time and must have fallen into a deeper sleep than I realized.

It was a little after 3:00 AM when I felt the cold steel of a pistol against my temple. A masked thug hovered over me in the darkness. "Get up. Slowly."

10

The masked thug backed away, keeping his distance as he motioned me out of bed. He'd taken my pistol from the nightstand.

He was a big, burly guy—6'3" and thick with dark eyes.

Commotion filtered down the hallway. The intruders had already been in Madison's room and rousted her out of bed.

My heart thudded, and adrenaline coursed through my veins. I carefully climbed out of bed and stood up with my hands in the air.

The pale moonlight filtered in through the floor-to-ceiling glass doors that led to the balcony.

With his pistol, he motioned me into the hallway.

There were two more thugs. One with a medium build and light eyes that stood about 5'11". He had a gun to Madison's head. The other skinny one stood nearby, fidgeting nervously. He was maybe 5'9".

They all wore black ski masks and black clothing.

"What do you want?" I asked.

"We just came for one thing," 511 said. "Don't cause any trouble, and we'll be out of your hair in no time."

They marched us down the hall into an office area. There was a glass desk, a few leather chairs with chrome piping, and a few boxes in the corner that still needed to be unpacked. Another large window offered an expansive view of the mountains. Elegant wood paneling accented certain walls, and exposed beams in the ceiling added contrast to the stonework.

"Who are you?" 511 asked me.

"Who are you?" I replied in a moderately snarky tone.

He got aggressive and moved away from Madison while Skinny kept an eye on her. He stormed closer with the barrel aimed at my head. Still not close enough to strike. Those moves were risky anyway. "I'm asking the fucking questions here. You a boyfriend?"

"No. I'm her brother."

"Where's the husband and the kid?"

"Like you don't know."

His brow knitted behind the mask. "You'd better start cooperating with me."

"They've been kidnapped," I said.

"Bullshit."

"It is what it is."

"Is anybody else in the house?"

"You're looking at everybody."

It was clear in my mind that 511 was Quentin. He matched the description, at least from what I could tell. He had a scar across his upper lip, perhaps from a fight or an accident. It was visible through the mouth hole in the ski mask. An identifiable feature. He should have covered it.

Quentin moved to a large wood panel on the wall, pressed it, and it clicked open. He swung it wide, revealing a safe behind the hinged panel. It was a clever secret compartment.

The safe was pretty standard—keypad entry, LED status lights, and a brushed nickel handle.

It was large enough to house documents, jewelry, and various other items. Maybe 16x16.

I glanced at Madison. She looked astonished. I don't think she knew it was there.

Quentin punched a code into the keypad. The LED light atop the digits flashed red.

"Fuck!" he muttered, then punched in the code again.

It flashed red a second time.

"Mother fucker!" he muttered under his breath.

He spun around, marched to Madison, and put his pistol against her forehead.

She gasped, and her terrified eyes rounded.

"What's the code?"

"I don't know."

"Bullshit!"

"I didn't even know there was a safe!"

"Keep lying to me. See how far it gets you."

"I'm not lying," she said, on the verge of tears.

This was all too much for anybody to handle. First, her family was kidnapped. Now this? She was on the verge of a breakdown.

Quentin tensed and tightened his grip on the pistol. The barrel pressed hard against her skin. "You have 10 seconds to tell me the code, or I'm going to blow your fucking head off."

11

"I don't think you want to do that," I said.

"Why is that, tough guy?"

"Because you could get on my bad side, and you don't want to be on my bad side."

He laughed. "I don't give a fuck about you or your bad side, Buddy."

"We ain't buddies."

He marched toward me and shoved the twitchy barrel in my face. "Maybe I'll shoot you instead if she doesn't start talking."

"I don't know the code!" Madison cried.

"Then maybe I should just shoot you both," Quentin said.

"I can get into that safe," I declared. "You can have whatever's in there. Neither of us care. But once you get what you want, you have to leave. I don't know who you are or where you came from. You get what you want, you can walk out of here, and we never have to cross paths again."

I wasn't about to let on that I knew who Quentin was. It might force him to think he had no options other than to give us an early exit from the world.

Quentin considered the offer for a moment. "Well, what are you waiting for? Get in the safe."

"I need a few items."

"Like what?"

"A coat hanger."

He laughed, then said in disbelief, "You're gonna break into a safe with a coat hanger?"

"Yep."

He stared me down for a moment, then exchanged a quick glance with his comrades.

They were out of options at this point. They just shrugged.

"Okay, tough guy. You'll get your coat hanger. But if you don't get into that safe, I'm shooting you first. Then I'm going to do really fucked up things to your sister. Who knows, she might even like it."

My jaw clenched, and my hands balled into fists. Quentin had definitely gotten on my bad side.

The punk nodded to his comrades, and the skinny one darted out of the room and rummaged through the house, looking for a coat hanger. He came back with a thick plastic one.

I looked at him like he was an idiot. "No. A wire one."

"Oh. Hang on a minute."

He spun around and darted out of the office. He made a ruckus rummaging through the closet in Madison's bedroom. He returned a few moments later with a cheap wire coat hanger. "Like this?"

"Perfect."

He approached cautiously and held out the coat hanger, keeping his distance. As soon as I grasped it, he backed away.

Quentin glared at him, not impressed by his skittishness.

I figured him for the least experienced of the bunch.

The big guy remained stoic. Something told me he was the dangerous one. Quiet, calm, unflappable. Capable. Quentin was a hothead. Acted on impulse. Quick to anger.

I tried to formulate how I could use their various personality types to my advantage.

I unwound the coat hanger, straightened it out, then approached the safe. I'd broken into these kinds of things numerous times. They were terrible designs, meant to look impressive. But they couldn't keep a professional out. If you wanted to hide stuff from your family members or just have a place where you wouldn't lose important papers, these things served their purpose. But if you wanted real protection, they were worthless.

With all the running around and the nerves, Skinny had gotten hot. He peeled off his jacket and tossed it on the floor. A silver chain glimmered around his neck, barely visible.

On his wrist, a silver bracelet in the shape of a serpent eating its own tail—an ouroboros.

"Hurry it up," Quentin barked.

I used the tip of the wire to poke out the LED above the keypad. It was attached to a circuit board that was glued to a sponge affixed to the door. It popped out relatively easily. Then I bent the coat hanger at an angle and reinserted it through the tiny LED hole, and used it to actuate the solenoid.

With a click of the handle, I was in the safe.

I swung the door wide and looked inside. I had to admit, I was anxious to see what all the fuss was about.

12

Quinton's eyes rounded as he approached the safe. His whole body stiffened, and he flew into a rage, his cheeks red, his veins bulging. "Where is it!?"

He trembled with anger.

The safe was empty.

He asked again in a low growl. "Where. Is. It?"

"I don't know," Madison declared.

Quentin did something stupid. He moved closer and put the gun to my temple. "Tell me where it is, or your brother gets a bullet through his brain."

This was a bad situation. No amount of slick moves or lightning-fast reflexes would get me out of the situation. It was too risky. The other two goons would react before I had a chance to disarm Quentin, and Madison could get hurt.

"It was in here," Quentin said. "The old man was the only one with the combination to the safe. Where is it?"

"Maybe he moved it," I suggested in a dry tone.

"He died. Nobody else had the combination."

"He either moved it, or somebody else had the combination," I said.

His grip intensified. "Somebody better tell me where it is, or I'm going to pull the trigger. I'm going to count to 10. One..."

Madison's frantic eyes found mine.

"Two..."

"I moved it," she said.

"Now we're getting somewhere," Quentin replied. "Where is it?"

I didn't know if she was bluffing or if she really had moved it, whatever *it* was.

"It's in a safe deposit box at the bank."

Quentin groaned. "Why is it there?"

"Because it seemed safer."

Quentin glared at her.

"You saw how easy it was to breach the safe," Madison said.

Quentin removed the gun from my head and paced around the room, thinking about it. He facepalmed, looking distraught.

"I say we get outta here," the skinny guy said.

"Shut up," Quentin snapped.

"Look, let's take the jewelry or whatever else is valuable in the house and go," Skinny said.

"Shut up!"

"Nobody's going anywhere," the big guy said in a cool voice. "We're going to get what we came for."

He meant business.

Quentin paced around the office for a moment, then said to Madison, "Here's how this is gonna work. We're going to go to the bank as soon as it opens. You're going to get it out of the safe deposit box and give it to me. If anything goes wrong in the process, my people are going to kill your brother. Is that clear?"

Madison's face tightened, and she swallowed hard. She nodded.

"Good. If you alert anyone in the bank or cry out for help, I swear to God, he's dead."

Madison nodded again.

I figured Madison was bluffing her way through the whole thing. I knew her well enough to know her *tells*. There was nothing in a safe deposit box, but the ruse would buy us a little bit of time. Dying in a few hours from now was better than dying now.

I had to admit, the goons were somewhat prepared. They'd brought rope, duct tape, and they all wore gloves. They tied us to the chairs in the office and waited until morning.

The big guy remained stoic, keeping a watchful eye. Quentin paced around nervously, and the skinny guy fidgeted, making numerous trips to the bathroom.

Morning light filtered through the windows. It was still overcast, and the mountain was covered in a blanket of fog.

I struggled against my bonds for two hours, trying not to draw attention to myself, but I wasn't going anywhere. The rope was tight, and I hadn't been able to work in any slack.

The bank opened at 9:00 AM, and Skinny fixed breakfast for the crew. They had no problem making themselves at home.

Finally, the time had come. The big guy untied Madison, and Quentin escorted her toward the door. "Take a good, long look at your brother. This is the last time you'll see him alive if you try anything funny."

I gave it a 50-50 chance that they'd let us live if they got what they were looking for.

Madison's terrified eyes gazed at me one last time before Quentin ushered her out of the room.

13

I t seemed like an eternity while Madison was gone. My
stomach twisted in knots. Every second wasted in this
chair was a moment lost in the pursuit of the kidnappers. If we didn't get out of this situation, I feared the worst.

It was close to 10:00 AM when Skinny's phone buzzed. He
hissed, "What's taking so long?"

I couldn't make out clearly what was said on the other end
of the line. It had to be Quentin. Who else would it be? I
figured these guys were carrying one-time-use burner
phones. I mean, who'd be stupid enough to take calls on
their own cell phone?

Skinny listened intently. "That's great." Then he said to the
big guy, "He's got it."

At this point, I knew something was up.

Skinny continued listening as Quentin barked into the
phone. "He wants us to meet them at the rendezvous point."

"What about him?" the big guy asked, nodding to me.

"He says to leave him."

"No. I'm not going anywhere until I see it."

Skinny looked confused. "What's the big deal?"

"The big deal is, I'm not going anywhere until I see it personally."

Skinny hesitated.

"Give me the phone!" The big guy snatched it from his grasp and grumbled into the phone, "Where are you?"

Quentin replied.

"I'm not leaving here until I'm sure we got what we came for. Bring the girl back here."

Quentin responded.

"I don't care what you think. We're doing it my way. These two are witnesses, and I'm not going to jail."

Quentin said something else.

"I don't care. I'll do them both. But I want to see it first."

Then Quentin said something that upset the big guy.

"You do that, I will find you. You understand?"

I figured Quentin had threatened to take off with the loot and ditch these two idiots.

"You'd better get here in 10 minutes. That's all I'm going to say." The big guy ended the call and handed the phone back to Skinny.

"What's going on?"

"What's going on is we're about to get screwed out of this deal," Big Guy said.

The doorbell rang.

The thugs froze for an instant.

"Who the hell is that?" Skinny asked.

"How the fuck should I know?"

The bell rang again.

"Go see who it is," the big guy commanded.

"You want me to answer the door like this?"

"No, stupid. I don't want you to answer the door. Just see who it is."

Skinny darted out of the room, and the big guy glared at me. "You expecting anybody?"

"No. Maybe it's your friend."

"He wasn't that close."

My phone buzzed the nightstand in my guest room. The vibration filtered into the office. I figured it was JD. He said he'd be here in the morning. I figured he'd probably stayed out all night with the band, hopped on the red eye, and slept the entire way.

Skinny darted back into the office. "Some dude with long hair. Looks like that guy in that '80s rock band. What was his name?" Skinny said, trying to remember something well before his time.

Outside, Jack banged his fist against the heavy oak door.

"He's not alone," Skinny said, panic in his voice. "There's a black Yukon in the driveway. There's a guy behind the wheel. Might be somebody else in the vehicle."

The big guy grumbled under his breath. "Keep an eye on him," he said, motioning to me before darting out of the room.

Skinny shifted nervously.

JD kept banging on the door.

The big guy returned a moment later. "Let's get the fuck out of here. There's several of them."

Big Guy pulled a silencer from his pocket and screwed it onto the end of the threaded barrel.

Skinny's eyes rounded. "What are you doing?"

"No witnesses." The big guy approached and aimed the pistol at my forehead.

"He hasn't seen our faces," Skinny said. "He doesn't know who we are?"

"I'm not taking that chance."

14

The big guy's grip tightened around the trigger, the deadly barrel staring me down.

A spike of adrenaline rushed through me like an electric current. My heart pounded.

"No," Skinny hissed. "Don't do it."

"Fuck you."

"I don't want to go down for accessory to murder."

JD twisted the handle and pushed open the heavy oak door. Quentin must have left it unlocked when he left with Madison. "Anybody home?"

Jack's voice echoed through the foyer and drifted upstairs.

It was enough of a distraction to interrupt Big Guy's progress. JD was a more immediate threat.

Big Guy exchanged a glance with Skinny, then moved to the door. He peered into the hallway.

JD shouted again. "Anybody here?"

"Two intruders," I yelled. "Armed. Upstairs!"

That didn't go over well with the two thugs.

The big guy hesitated in the doorway for a moment. He looked like he wanted to come back and put a bullet in my head. But with JD advancing to the base of the stairs, he thought better of it. He darted across the hall into another guest room and slid open the balcony door. He hustled outside, hopped the railing, and dropped down into the snow.

Skinny remained paralyzed.

"Now's your chance," I said. "Better get while the getting's good."

He hesitated a moment, his eyes round with fear. Then he darted across the hall and followed after his comrade.

When I was sure they were gone, I shouted. "I'm in the office. It's clear."

JD entered a moment later, holstered his pistol, and rushed to untie me from the chair.

I told him how the thugs had exited.

He darted to the balcony, peered over, but the goons were long gone.

JD stepped back into the office as I finished getting myself free from the chair.

"I see you're making friends already," Jack said. "What the hell happened?"

I filled him in on all the details.

My wrists were red and grooved from the tight ropes—my hands practically numb. I hustled into my guest room and dialed Dakota.

"You're okay," she said, surprised. "I'm just pulling into Madison's. We've got Quentin in custody. He sent her into the bank alone. She went straight to the manager and reported the issue. They called my office, and we picked him up outside the bank, sitting in her car. He didn't really think this through."

"Is Madison okay?" I asked.

"She's a little frazzled, but she's just fine."

"I take it Quentin didn't get what he was after."

"I'm still not sure what he wanted," Dakota said.

I hustled downstairs and stepped outside as they pulled up the driveway and parked in front of the house.

Jack's driver was still in the black Yukon, along with the guys in the band. They hopped out and greeted me.

"Yo, what's up, man?" Crash said, giving me a handshake and a bro hug.

"Long story."

"I saw JD draw his weapon and push inside. We figured it would probably be best if we stayed in the car."

"Smart move. What are you guys doing here?"

"Shit, we came for moral support, bro. We heard about the situation," Crash said with sad eyes. "Really sorry, man."

Madison and Dakota hopped out of Dakota's patrol vehicle. It was a green and white SUV with the Alpine County logo on the door with mountain peaks in the background and the slogan: *Securing the Wild West Since 1880!*

The two approached. Madison ran into my arms and gave me a hug.

"Are you okay?" I asked.

She nodded.

"You did good," I assured.

"Did you get a look at the accomplices?" Dakota asked.

"I can give you a physical description, but that's about it."

"Quentin is getting processed right now. I figured you'd want to have a talk with him."

"You got that right," I said.

"You think he's involved in the kidnapping?"

I shook my head. "No. I think this was pure coincidence."

I escorted Madison inside, and the band unloaded their gear from the SUV and followed us in.

JD greeted us in the foyer. "Been a long time."

Madison nodded and gave him a hug. "Too long."

"This is my band," JD said. "The mighty Wild Fury." He introduced Crash, Dizzy, and Styxx.

The long-haired rockers exchanged pleasantries.

"Don't worry, we've got a place to stay," JD assured. "We just can't get in until this afternoon."

"You could have stayed here. I've got plenty of room," Madison said.

"I see that."

"Nice place," Crash said. "We're really sorry about what happened."

Madison gave a grim smile and nodded.

The rest of the guys offered their condolences as well.

I reminded everyone that we were going to get Amaryllis and Flynn back. No need for condolences just yet.

"Where are you staying?" Madison asked.

"Coyote Creek Lodge. They had a cancellation."

"Fancy."

JD smiled. "I know."

We had stayed there last year during our adventure. The place was epic. I'm not sure who owned it at the moment. It was in a state of flux when we left, to say the least.

Tara pulled up in her white Mercedes GLA. She hopped out and gently knocked on the door before entering. Her big blue eyes took in the crowd. "I hope I'm not interrupting anything. I just thought I'd stop by to check on you. I tried calling, but no one answered."

"It's been an *interesting* night," Madison said.

She introduced Tara to the gang. They were all instantly smitten.

"If you'll excuse me," Madison said. "I'm going to check my cell phone. There's no telling what else I missed."

Madison hustled upstairs.

The guys in the band couldn't take their eyes off Tara.

"You like rock 'n' roll?" Crash asked.

She shrugged. "Yeah, sure."

"You should check out our show. We're playing at Silver Rush."

"You booked a gig?" I asked.

"Why not?" JD said. "Makes the trip a tax write-off."

A moment later, Madison shouted. "Tyson! Come here! The kidnappers responded."

15

The kidnappers had texted a short video.

It was hard to watch.

Amaryllis looked unharmed but clearly upset and crying. Without cutting, the camera panned to Flynn. He was bound and gagged. Today's paper was placed in frame to give the date.

The clip ended.

I watched the video a few times, trying to glean as much information as I could from the surroundings, sounds, and visible information. It looked like they were in a cabin in the area somewhere. But there wasn't much to go on.

I forwarded the clip to Isabella so she could work her magic, analyzing the metadata. Maybe there was something in the file that could lead us to their location. Cameras often record GPS data and embed it into the video, along with device information, time, and other details. I didn't think kidnappers would be that stupid, but it was worth a shot.

Madison's phone buzzed a moment later.

"Hello?" she answered in a timid voice. She put it on speaker.

"We sent the proof of life that you requested. You have 72 hours to transfer the money. You'll be texted a crypto wallet address."

"I don't have a crypto account," Madison said. "It's going to take time to set one up and transfer the funds. 72 hours isn't enough time."

"It's all the time you've got."

I took over the call. "You're not getting anything unless we make an exchange in person."

There was a long silence.

The distorted voice answered a moment later. "You're not making the rules here. We are."

"If you want the money, you play by my rules."

Madison glared at me.

"You've been snooping around, asking questions. You've involved local law enforcement. We told you not to do those things. There will be consequences if you keep pursuing this investigation."

"There will be consequences if anything happens to either Amaryllis or Flynn," I said through gritted teeth.

"And because of the trouble, the ransom is now $15 million. Keep playing games, and the situation will get more and more expensive."

The caller disconnected.

I wanted to tell the guy just how expensive this was going to be for him when I caught up with him. He was gonna pay for this in blood.

Madison took the phone from my hand. "I wish you wouldn't be so antagonistic."

"Are you gonna pay them the money?" Tara asked.

"I don't care about the money," Madison said.

"I don't mean to pry, but do you have that just lying around?"

"It's accessible."

Tara whistled. "Wow! Must be nice."

Madison snapped at her. "There's nothing nice about this situation."

"I'm sorry. I didn't mean it the way it came out."

Madison softened. "I understand. Sorry. I'm just on edge."

Tara gave her a hug. "Everything's gonna be fine. They're not gonna hurt her. I promise."

"Don't make promises you can't keep," Madison said, tears spilling over.

"Do you need help setting up a crypto wallet?" I asked.

"No. I've got one. I just wasn't going to tell them that. I was trying to buy us time."

"Good thinking."

The burglars had taken my pistol. I took my backup from Madison. JD said he would stay with her while I went with Dakota to the station to interview Quentin. I told him to walk the perimeter and secure the house. I figured Quentin and his gang got in through a second-story window or balcony that wasn't locked. I had checked everything except Madison's balcony. When she had stepped onto the balcony to smoke a joint, she'd probably left the sliding glass door unlocked.

We left the house, and I hopped into Dakota's patrol unit. We drove down the mountain, heading toward the station.

"You're not having the best of luck this trip," Dakota said.

"Let's hope things turn around, and soon."

The small department bustled with activity. Desk jockeys answered phones, and dispatch coordinated with patrol units. The patrol division responded to minor criminal incidents, civil complaints, and emergency medical calls. Home invasions and kidnappings were unusual for the posh resort. Under her watch, Dakota had expanded the department somewhat, but it was far from a big operation.

We joined Quentin in a small interrogation room. A hanging lamp illuminated the table, casting an ominous glow on the suspect below. We took a seat across the table from the scumbag. He was mid-30s with blue eyes, short wavy dark hair, and a shifty demeanor. A day's worth of stubble lined his square jaw. He'd been there long enough to sweat, even though it was crisp and cool outside.

I smiled. "This is the part where you get to rat out your accomplices."

He looked at me for a long time before speaking. "What's in it for me?"

I exchanged a glance with Dakota.

"I'll talk to the DA," she said. "I'm sure we can work out some type of reduction in sentencing if you cooperate."

I didn't think he had any involvement in the kidnapping of Flynn and Amaryllis, but I pressed the issue just in case. "Tell me everything you know about Amaryllis and Flynn."

"The kid and the husband?" he replied. "You said they were kidnapped. I didn't have anything to do with that."

"Maybe you've got other accomplices," I suggested.

"Only the two that were with me. We weren't gonna hurt anybody. I just wanted to get what was mine. I asked nicely. That bitch wouldn't let me in the house."

"I would take care how you refer to people," I warned. "Your friends didn't share your nonviolent approach."

His eyes flicked between the two of us. "What do you mean?"

"The big guy didn't want to leave any witnesses."

Quentin swallowed hard. "Nobody was killed, were they?"

Sweat misted his skin.

The penalties for kidnapping were steep. Quentin had certainly kidnapped us. Adding murder to a kidnapping charge wasn't much of an addition, but I let him sweat it out.

"Names," I said. "I want names."

The muscles in Quentin's jaw flexed as he contemplated it.

"What's the difference?" I asked. "I mean, you're going to jail for a long time. Maybe that stay can be shortened. Meanwhile, they'll be on the outside, living the good life."

He thought about it for a moment but said nothing.

"What were you after?" I asked.

"I ain't telling you shit. I want to talk to a lawyer. Now!"

That was the end of the interview.

"Let me tell you this. If you know anything about the kidnapping, and you don't tell me, I'll find a way to make your life miserable."

"My life already is miserable."

I leaned in and stared him down. "You have no idea what misery really is."

Fear crept into his eyes for a moment. He'd been to prison before. He knew exactly what was in store for him. He survived five years, and he figured he'd survive whatever was in front of him. But he was in for a long stretch.

Dakota and I pushed away from the table and stepped into the hallway.

"You think the other two will come back?" Dakota asked. "Try to get whatever it is they're after?"

"I wouldn't put it past them."

"And you have no idea what that is?"

I shook my head.

A deputy approached. "Sheriff, you're not gonna like this. Ray Bishop was ice-fishing at Alpine Lake. He found a..." Her voice quivered, and she cleared her throat. "He found a body in the snow."

Dakota lifted the surprised brow, and her eyes rounded. "Who?"

16

I rode with Dakota in her patrol car to Alpine Lake. It wasn't easily accessible. Maybe the dead body was related, maybe it wasn't. But I thought it was worth checking out.

Two of her deputies followed.

I had my own adventure in the area before. It was a mile or so off the highway and required a vigorous trek through the wilderness. Depending on the amount of snowfall and the temperature, it could be quite daunting. But once you arrived, you were rewarded with a pristine lake nestled amid snow-capped peaks and tall evergreens. It wasn't far from an old historic cabin.

The medical examiner met us in the parking area at the mouth of the trail. We were joined by an emergency medical crew and the local news.

Pierce Everett hopped out of the news van with his crew. He was a distinguished-looking gentleman in his mid-40s with wavy dark hair, narrow blue eyes, and that television square jaw. He and his crew hustled toward Dakota as she stepped out of the patrol unit. "Sheriff, what can you tell us about the incident?"

The camera closed in, and the sound guy hovered a fluffy boom microphone overhead.

Dakota looked at him like he was an idiot. "As you can see, I haven't been to the crime scene yet, so I can't tell you anything about it."

Pierce frowned.

The trail had seen some foot traffic in recent days. There hadn't been a lot of fresh snow, so it was a relatively worn path. We marched through the trees. The sharp air and spicy scent of evergreens swirled.

A doe and two fawns took notice of us about halfway down the trail. They looked on with curiosity for a moment before darting into the thick foliage and disappearing.

I was still wearing the same outfit from yesterday, and this was not the environment to wear sneakers. It didn't take long before my feet were freezing and damp from the icy snow. I needed a new wardrobe, and pronto.

The frozen lake looked mystical with the mountains presiding above. Small fissures in the ice created geometric patterns. The wind had blown snow drifts along the bank and around rock formations. Gray clouds loomed overhead, and a haze hung in the air.

Ray stood by his fishing hole in the ice.

"How thick is that ice?" I muttered.

Dakota shrugged. "Should be pretty solid this time of year."

It was always risky.

She took a cautious step onto the ice.

It didn't give way.

She took another and kept creeping forward.

The trick was going to be getting across the ice without busting my ass again. It was frosty in areas and slick in others. Bits of snow crunched under the soles of my shoes as I took cautious steps.

Ray was in his early 60s. He had a stark white beard and mostly silver hair with a few streaks of dark brown. He had a bulbous nose, and a worn face. He was bundled up and well-prepared for the elements. There was a folding chair by the hole he'd carved into the ice with a chainsaw. An ice chest sat beside the chair, along with a few fishing poles.

He greeted us and led us to the remains that were buried in a mound of snow by a rock formation that protruded from the surface, not far from his fishing hole. "I came out this morning, cut a hole in the ice with my chainsaw, and started fishing. I must have been out here a few hours before I noticed anything. I saw something in the snow. Figured I'd give it a look. As I got closer, I realized it was a strand of hair. Then I dug into the snow, and you can imagine my shock when that hair was attached to a head that was attached to a body. I called the department right away."

The medical examiner snapped on a pair of nitrile gloves and started brushing away the snow and ice.

"What happened to Earl?" I whispered to Dakota. He was the old examiner.

"He retired. Sandra came on about six months ago."

Sandra was early 30s with light brown hair, a narrow face, and a dry demeanor. Her excavation revealed the remains of a young woman.

The victim wore tight black leggings, fashionable sheepskin boots, and a stylish white puffer jacket that extended to the mid-thigh. The freezing temperatures had preserved the body well. There was no telling how long the victim had been here. She lay in the snow drift, partially exposed, her tangled hair twisted and matted, hiding her face.

Sandra brushed the woman's hair from her face, and I recognized the victim instantly.

"Is that...?"

17

T he news crew gasped.

"This must have happened last night after her broadcast," Dakota said.

Ember Hayes was a popular investigative reporter. I met her briefly last year. The beautiful young woman had long raven hair, mesmerizing blue eyes, full lips, and classic features. Now she was ghostly pale, and her skin looked like porcelain.

When she was alive, the camera loved her. And so did everybody else—except for the people who she did exposés on. She was an ambitious journalist trying to make a name for herself, and she'd done so, at least in Alpine Park. I'm sure she had aspirations of a national news career. With her looks and tenacity, that was almost a foregone conclusion —until now.

"We can talk to the TV station and find out when her last segment was taped," Dakota said.

Even though every news-gathering camera was digital these days, people still referred to it as tape. Old industry lingo dies hard.

"You have a time of death?" Dakota asked Sandra.

"Difficult to say. I'll know more when I get her back to the lab."

The cause of death was obvious. Two bullet holes in her torso made a compelling argument against natural causes. Her shirt was stained with crimson.

Sandra continued, "From what I can tell, it looks like she was shot in the back. Probably small caliber—9mm, maybe a .22."

I stepped forward, knelt down beside the body, and surveyed the remains. Sandra looked at me with annoyed eyes.

"Sandra, this is Deputy Wild. He's an outside consultant."

"9mm," I said with confidence, examining the exit wounds in Ember's chest.

I stood up and stepped to Ray. "Have you seen anyone else out here?"

"No, it's been dead quiet. Not many folks come out this way in the winter." He paused. "Look over here."

He showed us to a nearby area where the ice was chipped and cracked. It looked like someone had tried digging through the ice to no avail. "I think whoever was responsible tried to dump her in the lake but couldn't get through the ice. So, they decided to bury her in a drift until they could get back here with some cutting tools." He raised his hands innocently. "I mean, I'm no detective, but that's what it looks like to me."

Ray's assessment was spot on.

I muttered to Dakota. "Have your people search the area. Look for shell casings, blood splatter, etc. We need to figure out if she was shot here or somewhere else."

She nodded and relayed the order to the other deputies.

"Can you think of anybody who would want to put a bullet in Ember?"

"She liked to ruffle a lot of feathers," Dakota said. "You two would have gotten along."

Pierce and his crew soaked up the morbid footage. He stood in front of the camera with the scene behind him, already reporting. "In a tragic turn of events, the life of Alpine Park's beloved investigative journalist, Ember Hayes, has come to a violent and tragic end."

He tried to sound sincere and sympathetic, but something told me his main competition was out of the picture.

"Tell me about him," I muttered to Dakota.

"What do you want to know that isn't self-evident?"

I gave her a look.

"Pompous asshole. Got popped for DUI last year. Number two in the ratings behind Ember. A distant number two."

"I guess he's number one now."

"I guess so."

I decided to interrupt his take. I stepped into frame and started asking questions. I flashed my badge quickly. Just long enough for the gold to register. "Tell me about your relationship with Ember?"

Pierce looked flustered. He stuttered for a moment. "She was a colleague and a friend," he said, re-composing himself. "The community has suffered a terrible loss." He turned back to the camera. "We will continue on, upholding her spirit of integrity and the search for truth." He nodded to the lens and did his best impression of sincerity—that self-accomplished smug expression with narrow eyes and a tight mouth.

"How well did you know Ember?" I continued.

He turned back to the lens. "As you can see, this is a developing story, and my assistance is needed with the case. We'll report back shortly." He motioned to the cameraman to cut, but the cameraman had no such intention. He knew this could get juicy.

Pierce addressed me. "I'm in the middle of a segment, if you don't mind."

Dakota was at my side and growing annoyed at his evasiveness. "Just answer the questions, Pierce."

His face tightened, and he glared at her for an instant. "I've known Ember for a long time."

"Did you get along?" I asked.

"We had a mutual respect for one another."

"You're at competing networks," Dakota said.

"Where is this going?"

Dakota shrugged. "Your main rival turns up dead with two bullets in her, and you're on the scene to cover it at the same time we are."

"I have my ear to the ground. My finger on the pulse. I know what happens in this town as it happens."

I suspected that Dakota was dealing with her own departmental leaks. Either that or Pierce knew where to find Ember.

He surely wouldn't want to miss this story. Killers often return to the scene of the crime and linger around, inserting themselves into law enforcement's efforts. Partially to keep tabs on the investigation and partially to feel superior. Like they got away with something. Many killers are often narcissists. They think they're better than everyone else. Smarter. Sometimes it's that arrogance that leads to their downfall.

In the brief time that I had known Pierce, he seemed to fit the bill of a narcissistic asshole. That didn't necessarily make him a killer, but I'm not going to say I didn't derive some satisfaction from ruffling his feathers.

"Can you think of anyone who may have wanted to harm Ember?" I asked.

"Ember was a sweetheart. But if you found yourself at the tip of her spear, it could be a very uncomfortable position. I suggest you talk to her producer. See what kind of stories she was working on. We all try to dig up dirt. Sometimes people don't want their dirt uncovered."

"You own a gun?" I asked.

"I do not." His eyes narrowed at me. "Who are you?"

"He's a consultant with the department," Dakota said.

Pierce tensed. "I'm happy to help your investigation in any way I can. But I can assure you, I had no involvement in Ember's demise. I take no pleasure in this."

He took a little pleasure in it.

"Now, if you'll excuse me, I have a job to do." He returned to his camera crew.

"You don't waste any time getting under someone's skin, do you?" Dakota whispered as we walked back to the remains.

"Time is of the essence."

"I'm officially deputizing you."

I lifted a surprised brow. "What!?"

"You heard me. You're more familiar with this kind of thing than I am. I could use your help."

"No. My focus is getting Amaryllis and Flynn back."

"And you'll be able to do that more effectively as an Alpine County Deputy. I'll give you a badge and everything."

I considered it for a moment. "No. I can't get distracted."

"I need your help. And you need mine. You'll be able to accomplish more with local authority. You know I'm right."

"Madison will kill me."

"Madison will appreciate it when you get her family back."

I gave it another long, hard thought. "Looks like you got yourself a new deputy."

She smiled.

One of the deputies snapped crime scene photos, and Sandra and her crew bagged the remains and hauled them back to the vehicles.

A search of the area didn't turn up any shell casings or obvious blood spatter. But there was a lot of ground to cover.

On the trek back, I postulated a few theories. "You said your drug problem is back and as bad as ever. Maybe Ember was getting close to uncovering a smuggling ring."

"Maybe. But she wouldn't have had to uncover much. I can tell you who is behind the smuggling ring. Jericho Lewis."

"Why don't you do something about him?"

"Knowing who's behind something and having evidence to secure a conviction are two different things. You know that, Deputy."

I knew it all too well.

We hopped into her patrol unit and headed back to town. We kicked around a list of theories and possible suspects and settled on a place to start the investigation. I called Isabella and asked her to look into Ember's phone records, credit card receipts, and the location history on her cell phone.

18

"That's terrible!" Ember's segment producer said. "Are you sure it's her?"

Dakota gave a grim nod.

Mark Thompson shook his head in disbelief. "I've been trying to get hold of her all morning. It was highly unusual for her not to respond or come in."

He was mid- to late 40s with salt-and-pepper wavy hair, a little bit of stubble, brown eyes, and a square jaw. He could have been in front of the camera but chose the other side. It was the safer business move. On-camera personalities fluctuated. Behind the scenes had more stability.

"When was the last time you spoke with Ember?" I asked.

"Yesterday evening," he said as he thought about it.

The TV studio buzzed with activity. Production assistants scattered about, news anchors prepared for the next breaking segment.

We spoke with Mark in *Studio B*. The walls were painted flat black and an array of lights hung from a grid on the ceiling. Large broadcast cameras covered multiple angles, and the operators wore headphones, keeping them in constant contact with the show's director.

"Can you think of anybody who may have wanted to harm her? Anybody she had trouble with?"

A grim chuckle escaped his mouth. "There were a lot of people that didn't like Ember Hayes. Don't get me wrong, she was a wonderful woman, but let's just say she could be a bit... challenging at times."

"A strong personality?" I said.

"The strongest." A somber smile tugged at his lips as he thought of Ember. "She had a way about her. Never took *no* for an answer. Believe me, that could get old after a while, but I loved her for it."

"What was she working on?" I asked.

Mark glanced around the studio to make sure no one was in earshot. "What I'm going to tell you is confidential."

"Sounds juicy."

"Well, I'll just start with the stuff that's public knowledge. You know about her exposé on Alexi Romanov."

"Deputy Wild is in from out of town," Dakota said. "He's not current on local events."

"He's a billionaire developer. Let's just say that Ember's investigations didn't exactly paint him in a flattering light. So unflattering were her segments that he sued her and the station for defamation."

Dakota said, "There was some controversy about a recent land deal. He bought the old Crystal Chateau for three times what it was appraised at. There was a lot of speculation that he was laundering drug money."

"Real estate is expensive around here, but nobody pays more than they have to," Mark added.

"Unless you're trying to drive up the value and launder money," I said.

Mark continued, "And then there were the allegations she made against the mayor."

I lifted a surprised brow. "The mayor?"

"Nathan Lancaster. It's a touchy subject." Mark exchanged a look with Dakota.

"Whatever you would say to me, you can say to Tyson," the sheriff added.

Mark continued, "She accused the mayor, the city council, and others of abusing the subsidized housing program here."

"Subsidized housing?"

"Alpine Park is an expensive town. You're aware of that. We have some of the highest real estate per square foot in the country. Everyone wants to live here. That's great if you're a billionaire. But if you're a waitress in a bar or a public servant, you either need to take advantage of subsidized housing or live in another town 20 miles away. And even then, you might not be able to afford rent. The rich and famous need someone to cater to their every need."

"The tax base provides for subsidized housing for those who qualify," Dakota said. "You have to work in Alpine Park and be under a certain income threshold. It's how I can live here. Unlike some people, I'm not a millionaire."

"So, what was the issue?" I asked.

"Well, the income threshold is $1 million, which seems a little excessive. How many waitresses do you know pulling in a million dollars? Plus, the housing authority runs the lottery that selects applicants. Ember made allegations that the lottery wasn't completely random."

"The housing authority picked favorites," I surmised.

"That was Ember's allegation. And she had amassed evidence that some of the people who had been awarded subsidized housing were then subletting the properties as vacation rentals for 20 and 30 times what they were paying for rent."

"Let me guess, she accused the mayor and some of the city council members of taking advantage of that."

Mark nodded. "She hadn't aired the segment yet. She was still working on putting it all together and gathering evidence. But word had gotten out, and I got more than a few phone calls from Nathan and some of the others pressuring me to kill the story. They threatened the station. Said that if we proceeded, they'd cut off access to press conferences and would bar interviews with any city officials."

"That seems illegal and against the First Amendment."

Mark looked at Dakota with trepidation before answering. "The law around here is subject to certain factors."

He didn't have to explain. I could figure it out.

Dakota said, "There's a lot of pressure from influential people to run things a certain way. Look, it's their game, and we play on their field. You want to remodel your house, you need to get permits from certain authorities. Want to build an extension, you need a permit. Want to open a restaurant—"

"You need approval," I finished.

"Nothing gets done in this town if you are on the wrong side of the powers that be. And nobody wants to get on their bad side." Dakota paused. "I told you, this job was more about politics than enforcing the law."

"Want to challenge something in court, good luck finding a judge that's gonna side with you against somebody more influential," Mark said. "That's the way it is around here. People accept it. It's the price of admission. It's a small community, 200 miles from the nearest major metropolitan area. People think they can get away with things. And, for the most part, they can."

"But Ember challenged that," I said.

"You're damn right she did. I gotta give her credit. The girl had balls."

"Anybody else we should look into?" I asked.

"Well, I assume Pierce is on your suspect list, but I seriously doubt he had any involvement."

"He does stand to benefit," I said.

"They couldn't stand each other. But that's only because he had a desperate crush on her, and she rejected him in a pretty embarrassing way."

I lifted a curious brow. "A jealous rival spurned."

"People have killed over less," Mark said. "You'll have to forgive me—I have an active imagination. It's part of my job." He thought about it for a moment. "Oh, and she did have a stalker. Young kid. Early 20s. He'd hang out at the studio, show up on location, follow her around. That kind of thing. I think he's mostly harmless, but you know, kinda creepy," he said, making a cringe-worthy face. "You never know. Those guys can snap all of a sudden."

"You know the guy's name?" I asked.

He frowned and shook his head. "Might want to talk to her best friend, Kinsley Jacobs. They were thick as thieves. If anybody would know the intimate details of Ember's life, it would be Kinsley."

A production assistant rushed to interrupt. "We're live in five."

"Gotta run. If you'll excuse me."

"If you think of anything else, get in touch," Dakota said.

"I will," Mark replied before rushing off. He stopped mid-stride and turned back. "Oh, one more thing." In a hushed tone, he said, "I wouldn't normally discuss something of this nature, but in light of the circumstances, this could be relevant."

He had our full attention.

19

"Ember was involved with Sutton Eldridge," Mark said.

Dakota lifted a surprised brow. "I wonder if his wife knew about the affair?"

Mark shrugged. "Rumors were starting to swirl around here. That's all I know."

"You have confirmation of this?" I asked.

"We never talked about it directly. I tried to respect her privacy."

"Sutton Eldridge is a handsome man," Dakota said.

"And with a wife like Morgan, I can't imagine a reason to step out, but Ember certainly had qualities."

Dakota and I exchanged a glance.

"I'm thinking we need to track down Mr. and Mrs. Eldridge," she said.

Mark shrugged again. "I'll leave that for you to investigate."

He stepped away and resumed his duties.

We left the high-energy studio and stepped outside. We found Dakota's SUV and climbed inside. She tried calling Amber's best friend to get the skinny, but Kinsley didn't answer.

Dakota fired up the engine and pulled out of the parking lot. I asked Dakota to stop at a clothing store, and she took me to Alpine Outfitters. It was a high-end boutique filled with trendy winter wear.

I could have done with a budget *sports and outdoor* store, but they didn't have those kinds of places in Alpine Park.

The place was full of powder jackets, ski pants, boots, poles, goggles, skis, sunscreen, hats, jeans, long-sleeve shirts, T-shirts, thermal underwear, you name it.

I grabbed a couple pairs of jeans, some winter shirts, another jacket, a beanie, sunglasses, warm socks, and water-proof hiking boots.

I left the store significantly lighter in the wallet and wore some of my new clothes out. I still needed a shower, but at least my feet weren't damp and cold anymore.

We headed across town to the west end and took Canyon Crest up the mountain.

My phone buzzed with a call from Isabella along the way. "Bad news. I still haven't been able to track down the communication from your kidnappers. I looked at the meta-data from the video you forwarded. There is no identifying information. No GPS. Nothing. They were smart enough to strip that out." She sighed. "I looked into Ember Hayes. According to her phone history, she was at the Snowdrift Lounge last night until a little after 11:00 PM. She left the bar, then the phone took a trip toward Alpine Lake but went off the grid along the way. I'm assuming someone took the phone from her and shut it off, given the situation."

"If you get a chance, sift through her call logs and see if you can put together anything unusual."

"Already did. She got a lot of unreturned phone calls from Pierce Everett. His phone was at the Snowdrift last night, too. Might want to look into him."

"What time did he leave?"

"The curious thing is his phone went off the grid at 10:22 PM. Didn't pop back up until 5:05 AM."

I thanked her for the information and ended the call.

Dakota turned up a private drive and drove up to another palatial ski-in, ski-out chalet nestled amid snow-covered evergreens. We parked, hopped out, and banged on the front door.

Like many of the newer homes, it blended classic elements with a modern flare. Intricate stonework, exposed wood beams, large windows offering stunning vistas.

Sutton answered the door a few moments later. He was in his late 40s with subtle hints of gray around the temples and a trimmed goatee that had more gray in it than the rest of his light brown hair. He had an impossibly square jaw, narrow blue eyes, and an athletic physique. He greeted us with a smile. "Sheriff Skye, what can I do for you?"

"I'm not sure if you've heard the news. Ember Hayes has been murdered."

His eyes rounded, and his brow lifted. He was speechless for a moment. Then he regained his composure. "That's unfortunate. What happened?"

"That's what we're trying to find out."

"When did this happen?"

"The details are still lacking," Dakota said.

A mix of sadness and confusion tensed his face. "Do you have any leads?"

"We are putting the pieces together."

He nodded in a daze.

"Is your wife at home?" Dakota asked.

"No, she's on the slopes."

"I don't mean to be indelicate, but it's my understanding you were having an affair with Ember," Dakota said, just putting it out there.

Sutton's face wrinkled. "Where did you hear that?"

"In the course of our investigation."

"I'm sorry, but whoever gave you that information is misinformed."

He was lying. His reaction to the news of Ember's demise said it all.

We both gave him a doubtful glance.

"When was the last time you saw Ember?" I asked.

Sutton hesitated a moment. His eyes shifted between the two of us, then he admitted, "Last night, at the Snowdrift Lounge."

"Did you go together?"

"No. I told you, there was nothing between us. I happened to see her at the bar. I said *hello*. We had a drink, and that was it."

"Just one drink?"

"Maybe two."

"Kind of sounds like a date."

"It wasn't a date," he said, his jaw tensing.

"If it walks like a duck..."

He stared at me for a moment.

"Did you two leave together?" Dakota asked.

"No."

"Did you see her leave with anyone?"

"No. We had a brief exchange."

"Over two drinks," I said.

"Yes, then I left and came home to my wife." He paused. "If I was having an affair with Miss Hayes, I wouldn't meet her in a public place like the Snowdrift where everyone in town could see. That would be the fastest way to start rumors. The kind of rumors that I don't think my wife would appreciate."

"What were you doing at the Snowdrift?"

"I met a colleague to discuss a potential business deal."

"But Ember offered a better deal," I snarked.

"My meeting concluded. I saw Ember, said *hello*, and we discussed a few things."

"What did you talk about?"

"I fail to see how that's any of your business."

"Did she mention her plans after she left the bar?"

"She did not."

"Was she meeting anyone else there?"

"I don't know," he said.

"Was she there by herself?"

"She was alone when I saw her."

"So she went to the Snowdrift alone."

"Women go to bars alone all the time. Maybe she was hoping to meet someone."

"I don't think Ember was the type of woman that needed to trawl the local bar scene to find companionship."

"Maybe she was meeting a friend."

"Do you own a pistol?" I asked.

"No."

"What about your wife?"

He laughed. "I don't think Morgan has touched a gun in her life."

"Is she the jealous type?"

His eyes narrowed at me again. An annoyed breath flowed through his nostrils. "I told you, there was nothing between Ember and me. We were friends. That was the extent of our relationship."

"If you recall anything else about the evening, you know how to get in touch with me," Dakota said.

"I will. I certainly hope you find out who did this. She was a wonderful woman. Alpine Park has lost a valuable member."

He excused himself, and we returned to the SUV.

"He's lying," I muttered.

"Sure seems that way."

"Ember left the Snowdrift Lounge, got into a car with someone, and was driven out to Alpine Lake," I said. "My guess is she was shot out there and dumped. It wasn't a spur-of-the-moment thing. The fact that they tried to dig their way through the ice with a shovel means they had prepared, but they were morons and didn't prepare adequately."

"Let's see if anyone at the Snowdrift remembers seeing her."

20

The Snowdrift Lounge was a swanky cocktail bar with a large fireplace, soft leather seating, cozy ambient lighting, and top-shelf liquor, along with craft beer and whiskey. Not a bad place to take a date or unwind after a hard day on the slopes. An intimate bar where the music wasn't so loud you couldn't have a conversation.

The crowd was light this time of day. Dakota and I approached the bar and leaned against the counter.

"What can I do for you, Sheriff?" the bartender asked.

He was in his late 20s with dark hair and strong features. He stood about 6'1" with a muscular build.

"Were you working last night?"

He nodded. "Pulling a double again today."

"Do you remember seeing Ember Hayes?"

"Yeah, she was here."

"Was she with anybody?"

"She came in and sat at the bar, then she talked to Sutton Eldridge. They moved to one of the couches right over there," he said, pointing to the corner.

"Did they leave together?"

He shrugged. "I'm not sure. It got pretty busy last night. I don't think so." He thought about it for a moment. "I think he left before she did. But they never leave together."

I exchanged a curious glance with Dakota.

"This was a common meeting place for them?" I asked.

"They were in here a lot. It didn't take a genius to figure out there was something between them. But they tried to act like there wasn't."

"Do you have any security cameras around the property?"

He shook his head. "Our clientele don't like having their every move filmed. Especially when they're married." He paused. "What's going on?"

Dakota told him.

His eyes rounded. "No shit?"

"No shit."

"You don't think...?"

We shrugged.

"Did you see Sutton's wife here last night?" I asked.

"I've never seen her here. Maybe that's why those two choose to meet here. And Sutton always pays in cash."

"Any particular reason she doesn't come in?"

"She can't stand Celeste."

"She owns the bar," Dakota muttered to me.

"Do me a favor," I said to the bartender. "Ask around. Somebody had to see Ember leave."

The bartender nodded. "Will do. I liked Ember. She was always nice to me."

We left the Snowdrift and stepped outside. Cars rolled down the avenue, and pedestrians in heavy coats strolled the sidewalks.

"I don't know about you, but I'm getting kind of hungry."

I nodded.

"There's a good place just down the street," Dakota said.

We strolled the sidewalk, and I called Madison to check on her. "Any word from the kidnappers?"

"No. I'm still waiting on that wallet address."

"Let me know as soon as you have it. I'll put my people on it and see if we can trace it."

"Okay."

"They may wait till the last minute. How are you holding up?"

"My stomach is in knots. I'm totally freaked out, and it feels like I swallowed acid. Other than that, I'm surviving." She paused. "Have you found anything?"

I updated her on the situation. "I don't think these cases are related, but I'm helping the sheriff out."

"You took on another case!?"

"Helping local law enforcement is never a bad thing. I was out of my jurisdiction before. Now I'm operating in an official capacity. This will help us get your family back. Your family is my family, and I'm going to do everything I can. But there is nothing we can do in the meantime. It's a waiting game now."

"Okay," she said in a sigh.

"Let me know the minute you hear from them. Is JD still there?"

"Yeah. Want to talk to him?"

"Sure."

Dakota handed the phone to Jack. "Hey, what's up?"

I gave him the rundown and told him I'd be investigating a few leads with Dakota for most of the day.

"I'll stick around here until it's time to check in at the Lodge. Then I'll come back and stay with her."

"I appreciate it."

I thanked him and ended the call. I felt much better about running around town with Dakota while JD looked after Madison.

We strolled the block to the Ore House Grill. The place buzzed with the lunch crowd. Waitresses scurried about, and the clatter of conversation filled the air. Black and white pictures of miners hung on the walls. Images of ore carts, railways, and dank shafts. Grimy, tired faces. Pictures of pump stations and old generators. It was a throwback to the Old West. The air was filled with the smell of spices and grilled food.

A cheery hostess greeted us with a smile and ushered us to a booth. I suspected the sheriff got preferential treatment. There were several other people waiting to be seated. The badge *has* its benefits, especially in a small town.

We slid into the cozy leather seats of a high-backed booth. The hostess dealt out menus, and I perused the offerings. The menu was full of classic American cuisine—bone-in ribeyes with garlic mashed potatoes, cedar plank salmon served with risotto and drizzled with lemon butter, smoked sausage, venison medallions, and game hens served with grilled vegetables and wild rice. Free-range herb roasted chicken with roasted potatoes. Porterhouse steaks, seared and served with steak fries and creamed spinach. Sweet corn soup topped with fresh herbs. To finish it off, dark chocolate cake layered with velvety ganache and served with a side of vanilla ice cream.

Rustic wood beams spanned the width of the establishment, crossing the high ceilings. Vintage mining tools, lanterns, and other gear hung from the walls. A large stone fireplace provided warmth.

I went with the buffalo burger and sweet potato fries. Dakota ordered the roasted chicken.

"I was thinking we could talk to the mayor after lunch," I said.

Dakota looked at me with concerned eyes. "I know you like to do the whole *bull in the china shop* thing, but let's approach this with a little subtlety."

"So, that's how it is around here," I said, half joking.

She gave me a look.

"Nathan Lancaster is not above the law. Nobody is."

"But..."

"But nothing."

"He sure seems to be abusing his authority."

"Allegedly." She paused. "Look, you need all the friends you can get right now. What you don't need is the mayor making things harder for you. Storming into his office and accusing him of murder is not what I would call subtle."

"He's got a motive."

"As do a lot of people."

"So he's just going to get a free pass?" I said, antagonizing her.

"Nobody is going to get a free pass. We'll talk to him. I'm just saying, let's not shoot ourselves in the foot." She sighed. "In case you forgot, I live around here. I work with these people. I need solid, substantial evidence before making those kinds of allegations. I can't go into his office and just bully him into a confession."

"Whatever you say, Boss," I snarked.

She shot me another lethal look, then someone across the restaurant caught her eye. She muttered, "Oh, shit."

21

"Let me do the talking," Dakota hissed as a man in his early 60s approached.

He wore a blue suit and tie with a pale blue shirt. His wavy silver hair hung over his ears, and he had a bushy beard and eyebrows to match. They were a little out of control. His face was lined, and he had the rugged look of a man who spent his years on the mountain. But I doubted he did any type of real physical labor.

Dakota forced a smile. "Mayor Lancaster."

Nathan returned the smile. "How's my favorite sheriff?"

"I'm good." His eyes flicked to me, awaiting an introduction.

"I'd like you to meet Deputy Wild. He's consulting on a case."

We shook hands and exchanged pleasantries.

His blue eyes squinted at me, then they flashed with recognition. "Ah, yes. The deputy who brought down my least favorite sheriff. Alpine Park appreciates your expertise. What brings you back to town?"

"Just happenstance."

"He's assisting with the Ember Hayes case," Dakota added.

Lancaster frowned and shook his head. "Terrible tragedy. She was a bright star on the horizon. Her presence in this town will be sorely missed."

Spoken like a true politician.

"I hope you can bring her killer to justice," he continued. "I don't need to tell you that this kind of thing is not good for tourism."

"What was your opinion of Ember?" I asked.

Dakota glared at me.

"I thought she was resourceful, dedicated, captivating."

"It's my understanding she made some pretty serious allegations."

"That was her forte. She liked to stir up trouble where none existed. But then again, that's the news today. It's infotainment. One manufactured crisis after another." Lancaster smiled.

I smiled back. "So the subsidized housing scandal is a nothing burger?"

His smile faded. "Like I said, Deputy, Ember liked to stir up trouble. Perhaps that was her undoing."

"What do you mean?"

"I mean, she had a habit of pressing people's buttons. Maybe she pressed the wrong one. I trust that you will look into that," he said, glaring at Dakota.

"Absolutely," the sheriff replied.

"Good. Now, if you'll excuse me, I need to get back to the office." His eyes flicked back to me. "It was nice to meet you, Deputy Wild. If your previous experience in our fair town is any indication, I have no doubt you will get to the truth."

"That I will," I assured.

He smiled again and left the booth. Nathan greeted the manager on the way out, then had a few words with a cute hostess before stepping outside.

"What part of *subtle* did you not understand?"

I shrugged innocently. "I thought I was being subtle."

"Bull. China shop."

The waitress clanked down our plates, and we chowed down. The buffalo burger was good, and the fries crispy. After we filled our bellies, we walked back to the patrol car and set out to find Pierce. I wanted to confront him about his infatuation with Ember Hayes.

We stopped by the rival television station. They told us Pierce was on location, covering an ice sculpture competition. We left and headed to the town square.

The buzz of chainsaws filled the air, and ice chips sprayed as artists brought their visions to life from solid slabs of ice. Contestants worked at a fevered pace, using chisels and blowtorches to shape their creations.

Pierce stood in front of the madness, talking into the camera. "We are less than an hour into the annual competition, and things are already taking shape."

At this point, it was hard to tell what these blocks of ice would become.

"As you can see behind me, contestants are pouring their hearts and souls into their creations, and we anxiously await the manifestation of their visions. We will report back throughout the day as this story develops. I am Pierce Everett, and this is the news as it happens."

We approached the reporter as the scene cut. He stifled a groan when he saw us and forced a smile. "What can I do for you, Sheriff Skye?"

The cameraman kept rolling and filmed our interaction. He knew it could get juicy at any moment and wasn't going to miss a thing.

"We just have a few follow-up questions for you," Dakota said.

"I'm happy to help."

"Seems like you made a lot of phone calls to Ember," I said.

"We had a professional relationship. I would often call her to bounce stories off her and see what she was covering to make sure there wasn't too much overlap between us."

"Didn't look like she returned the calls."

He frowned at me.

"It's my understanding you had quite a crush on her. Understandable. She was an attractive woman."

"Our relationship was strictly professional."

"But that wasn't for lack of trying, was it?"

His jaw tensed. "I asked Miss Hayes out for drinks in a professional setting. I believe she misinterpreted my intent."

"Did you see her out last night?"

"No, I didn't."

I feigned confusion. "That's odd. You weren't at the Snow-drift Lounge last night?"

He hesitated a moment and swallowed. "Yes. I was there for a brief minute."

"What time did you leave?" I asked.

"I stayed till 10:30 PM or so."

"Where did you go afterward?"

"I went home."

"You didn't see Ember?"

"No, I didn't. The club was crowded."

"Are you sure you didn't see her leave? Perhaps you offered her a ride home. Maybe she got into the car with you, and you took her for a ride. She refused your advances, and maybe things got out of hand. Your professional reputation would be at stake if she went on set and said she was sexually assaulted."

The reporter's face twisted with horror. "What are you talking about?"

I shrugged. "She got in a car with somebody around 11:00 PM and ended up dead."

He glared at me, then looked at Dakota. "You can't possibly think his theory has any merit."

Dakota shrugged.

"This is total bullshit. I left that bar around 10:30 PM and went home. What you're suggesting is pure fiction. You can't prove any of it."

I always got suspicious when people challenged me to prove it. "Can anyone else account for your whereabouts last night?"

"After I left the bar? No."

"Do you own a gun?"

"You asked me that before, and I told you no."

Pierce noticed the cameraman was filming him. He growled, "Turn that damn thing off," he said, marching toward the lens, covering it with his palm.

The camera guy backed away and adjusted focus after Pierce shoved the lens. The cameraman shrugged and kept filming, holding the camera from his hip, trying to act inconspicuous.

Pierce knew better.

He turned his attention back to us. "This conversation is over. If you have any more questions, please talk to my attorney."

Then Pierce got a brilliant idea. He motioned for the cameraman to keep rolling, which he already was. The guy shouldered the rig, and Pierce went into newscaster mode. "Who exactly are you, and what gives you the authority to investigate a murder in this town and make wild accusations?"

"I've deputized him to assist in the investigation," Dakota said. "If you have a problem with that, you can take it up with me."

"What are his qualifications? It seems reckless to bring in an outsider to go off on some unhinged investigation."

He was trying to use his stature to turn the tables and intimidate Dakota.

"I can assure you, I am well within my authority to deputize anyone I see fit. And Deputy Wild has more experience with homicides than anyone else in this county. Your lack of cooperation with our investigation has raised suspicion."

Pierce fumbled all over himself. In a blustery voice, he said, "I've been cooperating. I've answered every question."

"Until you requested an attorney."

"Which is my right."

"I'm just saying it looks suspicious. Jealous colleague. An unrequited obsession that ends in a tragic murder. That's newsworthy, don't you think?"

"If you're looking for someone obsessed with Ember Hayes, look no further than Bennett Fraser."

"Her stalker?" I asked.

"Well, look at the super sleuth," Pierce mocked.

A crowd had gathered and seemed more interested in our confrontation than the sculpture contest.

Pierce became painfully aware that he was the center of attention, and it wasn't the kind of attention he liked. He glared at Dakota, then motioned for the cameraman to cut and stormed away.

Dakota chuckled. She muttered, "I don't like that guy. Never did."

"Do you know Bennett Fraser?" I asked.

22

D akota told me some interesting things about Bennett.

We caught up with him at his apartment on Frostwood Falls. It was a four-story brown building with stonework at the base, gated under-building parking, and surrounded by evergreens.

I banged on the door to unit #412. The peephole flickered as Bennett peered through.

He opened the door a moment later with nervous eyes. Bennett was in his late 20s with curly brown hair, brown eyes, and a nerdy demeanor. He looked distraught. His eyes were red and puffy, and it looked like he'd been crying. They flicked between the two of us. "What's going on?"

"We're here to talk to you about Ember Hayes."

He hung his head. "I can't believe she's gone."

Dakota and I exchanged a look.

"When was the last time you saw Ember?" I asked.

He shrugged.

"Did you see her last night?"

"No."

"Are you sure about that?"

He looked up at me. "I'm sure."

"It's my understanding you were harassing her."

"I wasn't harassing her," he said, his face twisting.

"That's not what I hear."

"This wouldn't be the first time you've gone overboard," Dakota said. "Two women have restraining orders against you. You've got previous charges for online harassment and stalking."

"Those were misunderstandings."

"Were you stalking Ember?" I asked.

"No!" he said with a scowl. "I wasn't stalking her."

"What do you call it when you follow someone around and show up at their place of employment?"

He frowned and said nothing.

"You need to tell me the truth. Your cell phone was off the grid last night after 9:00 PM. Where were you?"

"You pulled my phone records?"

I gave him an ominous look.

"My battery died. I was here."

"You sure you didn't show up at Snowdrift last night, force her into your car, take her out to the woods?"

His brow knitted. "No. I would never do something like that. I loved her." His eyes filled, and he wiped the tears away before they fell. He pulled himself together, and vengeance filled his voice. His tone was stone cold. "I find out who did this, I'm going to kill them."

For an instant, he had the eyes of a killer.

It was creepy.

"You should leave matters to my department," Dakota said. "We'll handle this."

"What are you doing to find her killer?"

"Interviewing people like you," I said.

Bennett glared at me. "Well, you're wasting your time. I didn't kill her."

He'd had enough of the conversation and closed the door.

I exchanged a look with the sheriff.

Her walkie talkie squawked. "Sheriff, there's been another incident at Apex Apparel. Hudson's demanding to speak with you."

"Tell him I'm on my way," Dakota said with a sigh. She looked at me. "You up for the slopes?"

23

A fter getting fitted for skis, boots, and polls at a rental shop at the base of the mountain, Dakota and I took the gondola up to the summit. It was still overcast, and snow flurries had started to fall. The views from the gondola on a clear day were spectacular. Today, all you could see was the slope below and skiers plowing through the moguls, swishing back and forth. The gondola dangled from the wire as we made our ascent, swaying gently with the breeze. As we neared the peak, it rumbled and shook for an instant. It was quite unnerving.

"Does it always do that?" I asked.

Dakota cringed and gave me a concerned look.

We glided up to the tram house, hopped out of the gondola, and grabbed our skis from holsters on the side of the unit. I stepped into the bindings with a click, and we polled away from the tram house along the ridge.

"Try to keep up," Dakota said with a wink before plunging down the slope.

Apex was the longest run on the mountain and took you all the way down to the plaza.

Dakota moved with style and grace, shifting her weight, arcing from side to side.

I followed after her. I hadn't been skiing since our last visit to Alpine Park.

We cruised down the slope, racing past evergreens to a small chalet near the summit that was home to *Apex Apparel*. We kicked off our skis, leaned them against the railing outside, and stepped into the warm air. If you made it to the top of the mountain and were lacking any wardrobe items, Apex Apparel had you covered. They had ski pants, powder jackets, gloves, sunglasses, caps, sunscreen, fanny packs for water, backpacks, ski boots, poles, and even a selection of skis. Of course, on the mountain, you paid double what you would in town, and what you paid in town was double what you'd pay online.

They had a captive audience.

Drifts of snow and ice filtered in from the door and quickly melted.

Dakota made her way to the register. The manager behind the counter had an angry scowl etched on his face. "You have got to do something about this."

"I'm doing everything I can," she assured.

"It doesn't seem that way. This is the third time this month. They walked in, grabbed as much as they could from the racks, and walked out. Took about $5,000 worth of merchandise. It's like nobody cares anymore. They do whatever they want, and nobody is going to stop them. I'm going to have to start locking everything down, but I don't have the manpower to unlock everything every time somebody wants to try on a powder jacket. Do you know what that's going to do to my sales over time?"

"Can you give me a description of the thieves?"

"Yeah. They all wore ski masks and ski attire."

"I suggest you hire a full-time security guard," Dakota said.

"I shouldn't have to do that. And what's a security guard going to do? Shoot them? Then I'll get sued for wrongful death. Look, the lease on this place is astronomical. I'm beginning to think maybe somebody doesn't want me in business here."

"Have you talked to Dalton?"

"He says he's going to beef up security on the mountain, whatever that means."

"Who's Dalton?" I muttered in Dakota's ear.

"He owns the mountain." Dakota asked the owner, "You want to file an official report?"

"Is it going to do any good?"

Dakota gave him a flat look. "I can't make any guarantees. But just get it on record. You'll need that for insurance purposes, anyway."

Dakota pulled out her phone and, through a portal on the county's website, helped him enter the report.

Afterward, we left and stepped outside.

"How long has this kind of thing been going on?"

"It keeps getting worse. Times are tight, and the county doesn't have the manpower. I think criminals have figured out this town is easy pickings. Believe me, I've been taking a lot of heat for it. This kind of thing has been plaguing the shops on Main Street. Now they're moving to the mountain." She thought about it for a moment. "Maybe your kidnappers are from out of town, and they decided that Alpine Park is a target-rich environment. I sure hope that's not the beginning of a new trend around here."

JD texted: *[I'm leaving to check into the Lodge with the guys. Tara is going to stay with Madison until I get back.]*

[Cool.]

Dakota and I skied down, caught a lift up to Summit Ridge, skied down, and tried to find Madison's house. It took a little doing, but we found the access trail and skied up to the back door.

We kicked off our skis, and I banged on the door.

Madison had been keeping the doors locked as I had asked.

Tara let us in a moment later.

We peeled off our boots, left them in the mud room, and stepped inside. Tara escorted us to Madison, who was trying to relax in the second-floor lounge.

I caught her up to speed on the day's events. She still hadn't heard anything back from the kidnappers.

I decided to take the opportunity to jump in the shower while Dakota kept Madison company. After I toweled off, I put my new clothes back on and rejoined them in the lounge. Madison was almost in a fugue state. The stress and lack of sleep had done a number on her.

"Don't go to that dark place," I said. "We're going to get them back."

She nodded, wanting to believe me but unsure. I didn't want to make promises I couldn't keep, but I tried to reassure her.

We waited for JD to return. He said he'd stand guard and let me know if they heard anything from the kidnappers.

I asked Dakota if she knew where to find Alexi. I doubted he was involved in the kidnapping, but he was worth talking to. A guy involved in money laundering would have his finger on the pulse of Aspen Park's criminal enterprises.

"I've got a good idea where he might be," Dakota said.

24

W e skied down the mountain as the sun dipped over the horizon. I grabbed my boots from a locker at the rental place, and we carted the gear back to Dakota's patrol unit and attached the skis to the roof racks. I figured I'd hang onto them while I was here. Being in a marked patrol vehicle meant you could park anywhere and get away with it.

The Powder Club was accessible from the slopes or from Black Bear Road. It was a private dining club with sweeping views of the slopes. Membership was expensive and exclusive, and the five-star restaurant boasted guest chefs from all over the world. Rain or shine, this is where you could find Alexi Romanov on a Friday evening.

Dakota pulled to the valet and parked in front of the entrance. She didn't hand over the keys. "We'll only be a moment," she said to the attendant.

We pushed into the restaurant. Smooth orchestral music filtered through speakers, and the clinks and clatter of silverware filled the air. The maître d' greeted us with an uneasy smile. We weren't exactly dressed for this type of place, and we weren't members.

That didn't matter. Dakota had the VIP pass.

The maître d' was a tall man with a bulbous nose, a narrow face, and a lack of hair on the top of his head. He wore a tuxedo and a bow tie. "Good evening, Sheriff Skye. How may I help you?"

"Looking for Alexi Romanov," Dakota said.

"He's in a private room with a group right now. Would you like me to let him know that you're here?"

Dakota smiled. "No. Just point me to his location."

The maître d' didn't like that idea but forced a smile and acquiesced. "Certainly." He flagged over a waiter and whispered, "Please escort the sheriff to the Summit Room."

The waiter led us through a maze of tables to the exclusive room. Our presence drew curious stares from the patrons.

A man in a light gray suit guarded the door. His muscles bulged the fabric, and his blue eyes focused on us as he whispered something. He had an earpiece and was clearly communicating with someone inside the private room. A man like Alexi would have security 24/7.

The waiter pulled open the door and ushered us into the private dining area.

Mr. Gray Suit stared us down but didn't interfere.

Inside, another man stood watch over Alexi and his entourage, not surprised by our intrusion.

Alexi sat at the head of a long table with a dozen guests. A gorgeous blonde sat at his side, wearing a sparkling black cocktail dress with a low-cut neckline that was quite distracting.

At the far end of the room, floor-to-ceiling windows offered a view of the slopes. The sun had long since vanished, and lights illuminated the night run. It was a striking view.

All eyes flicked to us.

"Mr. Romanov," Dakota said. "I'm sorry to interrupt. This will only take a moment of your time."

He looked annoyed but put on a pleasant face. Alexi stood up and acknowledged his guests. "Ladies, Gentlemen. If you'll excuse me for a moment."

He stepped aside to join us.

The conversation at the table resumed.

Alexi was in his mid-40s. He had a boxy head and slicked-back brown hair with a pronounced widow's peak. He had narrow blue eyes and a trimmed goatee and was impeccably dressed. He spoke with a slight accent. "What can I do for you?"

"I'm sure you've heard the news about Ember Hayes."

"I have. But please don't ask me to pretend that I'm upset about it. As far as I'm concerned, she was trash."

"She seemed to have the same opinion of you," I said.

His eyes flicked to me and narrowed. "I'm sorry, but we haven't been introduced."

"This is Deputy Tyson Wild," Dakota said.

I extended my hand, and he hesitated before shaking it.

"Ms. Hayes said false and defamatory things about me. I'm sure you can understand my displeasure with her antics."

"Displeased enough to put a few bullets into her?" I said, not pulling any punches.

Dakota gave me a look.

Alexi smirked. "I see you've been taking her reports at face value. You can't believe everything you see on TV, Deputy. It's all sensationalism. Faux outrage. That kind of thing sells."

"So, you're not a gangster who launders money for the Russian Mafia?"

Alexi laughed again. "I only wish my life was so exotic and glamorous."

"Seems pretty exotic and glamorous to me."

"I'm an investor. I run a venture capital firm. We launch star-tups, develop properties, and we're even expanding into celebrity endorsements and management."

"Whatever is profitable," I said.

"I have a healthy relationship with money, Deputy. Unlike most people."

I gave him a curious glance.

"Most people are afraid of money. They make excuses. They say money brings problems. They justify their meager exis-tence by decrying the rich and saying how horrible those people are. How unhappy. How miserable. My life is quite enjoyable, as you can see," he said, motioning to the table of guests.

It was filled with modelesque women in skimpy evening attire. Sparkling diamonds draped around elegant collarbones and dangling from delicate earlobes.

"Money, in and of itself, won't make you happy," Alexi continued. "You must find meaning. That is the challenge for us all. But money buys time and opportunity."

"I'm sure it could also buy the means to get rid of a pesky reporter."

He stared at me for a moment. "Did you come here to accuse me of something?"

"We're talking to everyone who was at odds with Ember," Dakota said. "Nothing personal."

"Can you tell me where you were last night?" I asked.

"I enjoyed a quiet evening at home with Olga," he said, motioning to the striking blonde seated next to him at the table.

She wiggled her fingers and smiled at us.

"You weren't anywhere near the Snowdrift?"

"No." His eyes flicked between the two of us. "If that's all, I would like to return to my guests and enjoy my evening."

"Certainly," Dakota said. "Sorry for the interruption."

"One last question," I said. "You wouldn't know anyone involved in kidnapping and extortion, would you?"

He just stared at me. "Good evening."

He returned to the table, and we stepped out of the private dining room.

"Subtle," Dakota muttered.

I frowned dismissively. "You hungry?"

"It's about that time."

"Let's get a table."

"I don't have a membership."

We returned to the maître d', and I said, "Table for two, please."

His upper lip curled with disdain. Before he could turn us away, I smiled and said, "Guests of Alexi."

25

Much to his displeasure, the maître d' seated us at a surprisingly good table with a wonderful view of the illuminated slopes. A delightful waitress in formal attire approached and introduced herself. Autumn was a cute blonde with her hair in a stylish updo with wispy golden locks dangling around her ears. She told us about the specials and took our order. I went with the Rocky Mountain medallions—petite filet mignon, grilled to perfection, served with creamy spinach and mushroom sauce. Dakota went with the same.

This was the kind of place where your glass was never empty, and if you dropped your fork, someone was there to offer you a new one before you even looked for your server.

I would have ordered a nice bottle of wine, but Dakota was in uniform and had a policy against it. The company, the view, and the food were enjoyable enough. The meal was fantastic. Tender and juicy. Melt in your mouth delicious.

We kicked around ideas about the two cases. We were halfway through the meal when a man approached with a disturbed look on his face.

Dakota stiffened.

"What's going on here!?" the man said in an accusatory voice.

It didn't take a genius to figure out this was Dakota's fiancé.

He was a handsome guy in his late 30s with short, light brown hair, hazel eyes, and chiseled features. A thin beard rimmed his square face. He was about 6 feet tall and athletic but not overly muscular.

"I'm having dinner with a colleague," Dakota said, somewhat annoyed. "Connor, I'd like you to meet Deputy Wild."

I offered my hand to shake, but he didn't accept.

"Can I have a word with you?" he hissed at her.

Dakota looked embarrassed. "Excuse me," she said before pushing away from the table and stepping aside.

They had a heated exchange while I continued to enjoy my meal. I couldn't help but overhear their discussion. So could a lot of other patrons.

"What are you doing here?" Dakota asked.

"I'm having a business meeting with Dalton."

Her brow knitted with confusion. "Why are you meeting with Dalton?"

"Why are you having dinner with this guy?"

"We're investigating a case, Connor."

"Looks like you're on a date."

"Look at me. Is this what I wear when we go on dates?"

His face tensed.

"You're making a scene. Go back to your business meeting. We'll discuss this later."

He glared at her.

"I'm not doing this here," she said in a low voice that was not to be trifled with.

Connor's eyes flicked to me before walking away.

Dakota returned to the table. "Sorry about that. He gets a little jealous sometimes."

"I've noticed."

"He's a really good guy. Just a little..."

"Insecure."

"At times."

"You should join him. I can finish my meal alone."

"I'm not going to let anyone dictate what I can and can't do. I'm having a meal with a colleague, and there is nothing going on between us."

"We do have a little history," I said, playing devil's advocate.

"If he doesn't trust me, what is he doing with me?"

"True."

We finished our meal, and I picked up the hefty tab and left a nice tip for Autumn.

Connor glared at us as we left the restaurant. Dakota's patrol vehicle was still parked out front where she left it. The valet wasn't too happy about it, but we climbed in and drove away. She took me back to Madison's house and dropped me off.

"I'll call you in the morning," she said. "Let me know if you hear anything from the kidnappers."

I nodded and hopped out of the car. "Hope you can patch things up."

She rolled her eyes.

I closed the door and stepped to the porch as she drove away. Madison and JD were in the first-floor lounge, watching TV, trying to occupy themselves.

"Any news?" I asked.

26

J D frowned and shook his head.

We had a drink and discussed the situation. He said the guys in the band had gone into town to hit the bars.

"I got it covered here," I said. "Go have fun."

"I'm having fun," JD said.

Pretty much wherever JD was, that was the place to be.

Madison's phone buzzed with a text. It snapped her out of her fugue state, and she snatched it from the coffee table like a viper strikes its prey. She read the text message with wide eyes. "It's them! They sent a wallet address."

JD and I hurried to her and looked at the display.

"What do we do now?"

I took the phone and forwarded the crypto wallet address to my phone, then sent it to Isabella. [See if you can identify the owner of the wallet.]

It was a long shot, but not impossible. It took authorities in New York six years to track down the identity of a fraudster through his crypto wallet. We didn't have six years.

"I just want to pay the ransom and get my family back," Madison said, her eyes brimming.

"If you transfer the money, you may never see them again," I cautioned. "But it's your call."

Her face twisted, wracked with torment.

"Let's try to set up a meeting. An in-person exchange."

Madison nodded.

I replied to the kidnappers. [You get the money when we make the exchange in person. Everyone must be alive and unharmed.]

There was no immediate response.

Madison was a ball of nerves.

An hour went by, and still no response.

Then two hours.

I told Madison to get some rest, but I didn't think she'd be able to get any real sleep. She excused herself and retired to her bedroom, but I'm sure she tossed and turned all night.

By the morning, we still hadn't heard back from the kidnappers. But I did get another disturbing call.

"Turn on the news," Dakota said.

I got in front of the TV and flipped through the channels until I found a local station. Pierce Everett spoke into the camera with a grim scene behind him. "In the tragic turn of events, the gondola at Alpine Park has collapsed. Several have been killed, and a few survivors have been airlifted to a level one trauma center."

The camera cut to the disturbing footage. The cable had snapped, and the mangled gondola lay in the snow. The chassis had crumpled into a deflated mess, and the plexiglass windows had cracked and fallen away.

Pierce interviewed a sobbing woman. "It was horrible. The gondola rumbled, and we heard this horrible snap. Then we were in free fall."

She burst into tears and sobbed. "My husband…"

Her throat tightened, unable to finish.

Somehow, she had managed to walk away from it. But she was one of the few.

It was a gut-wrenching scene.

"I'm about to head to the site," Dakota said. "You feel like tagging along?"

"Think your fiancé will get upset?" I teased.

"Shut up. I'll be there in a minute."

She arrived in Madison's backyard on a snowmobile 15 minutes later.

Madison said she was going to spend the day at the restaurant. "I need something to focus my attention on."

"Call me the minute you hear anything. Do you want JD to escort you there?"

"No. I'm fine."

I called him anyway and asked him to chaperone her as I hustled outside and hopped on the back of the snowmobile. I hung on, and Dakota twisted the throttle. The engine howled, and the biting wind swirled as we climbed our way up the moguls to the crash site.

First responders swarmed, and Pierce interviewed everyone he could. Debris lay scattered about the crash site, and the twisted gondola looked like a crushed tin can. It was a miracle anyone survived.

I thought back to the shimmy we felt yesterday. This was a clear incidence of neglect. It wasn't a question of *if*, it was *when*. It could happen to anyone. A roll of the dice. We could have been snarled amid the mangled remains.

My blood boiled.

We took in the chaos as responders swarmed. Crimson splattered the snow and mortified onlookers gathered. Emergency responders searched the area for anyone who may have been thrown from the gondola as it tumbled down the slope. The ski patrol had evacuated a few of the minor injuries while the rescue chopper handled those in dire need.

Dakota and I set out to find a staff member who could shed some light on the situation.

27

"The lifts are inspected before the winter season," Jim said. "Inspections are unannounced and conducted by an independent engineer contracted by the state. Mr. Callahan is a stickler for safety."

"Clearly," I snarked.

Jim frowned.

"When was the last time the gondola was checked?"

"We have a lot of lifts. Eight in total. One gondola, a high-speed quad, a high-speed triple, two quads, and three doubles. There are over 80 runs, miles of slopes, and a lift capacity of around 10,000 people an hour. It takes time to inspect every inch of cable adequately."

"That didn't answer my question."

"I can check the maintenance records and give you an exact time frame."

"Who's responsible for lift safety?"

"We contract out to a company that specializes in lift maintenance. Of course, we have a few in-house maintenance engineers, myself included, but the repair work is subbed out. The operations manager oversees everything."

"What's the company?"

"Alpine Sky Cable."

"Who issues the lift permit?" I asked.

"The Passenger Safety Tramway Board regulates all lifts in the state."

Jim's phone buzzed.

"Excuse me," he said, then took the call. "Hello?" He listened intently. "Yes, sir."

A voice crackled through the speaker.

"Yes. Absolutely."

Jim stepped away and tried to have a private conversation. He chatted for a moment, then ended the call and returned to us. "If you'll excuse me, I really should get back to it."

"We just have a few more questions," I said.

"I'm sorry. I've been told not to say anything else without our corporate attorney present."

Dakota gave him a card and told him to get in touch if he felt like talking.

"Something tells me we might not get a lot of cooperation," I muttered as he walked away.

It wouldn't be long before investigators from the tramway board were on the scene.

"Are you thinking what I'm thinking?" I asked Dakota.

"You're thinking that an accident like this doesn't just happen. There are warning signs."

"Warning signs that someone ignored," I said. "Or covered up. What if someone was about to expose that negligence?"

Dakota lifted a curious brow. "Like a reporter?"

I gave a grim nod.

We headed down the mountain to the corporate office at the base camp. It was pure chaos. The other lifts had been shut down, and the mountain closed. There would be no more skiing today, or for the foreseeable future, until this incident got squared away and properly investigated.

People died. Lawsuits were inbound. Neither the operations manager nor Dalton Callahan were available. They were in full damage control mode and were probably crafting a response.

We left the corporate office, and Dakota shuttled me back to Madison's house. It was bizarre to see the slopes so empty this time of day. She dropped me off in the backyard.

"We need to track down the engineer that was contracted by the state to do the inspections," I said as I climbed off.

"I'll dig into this and see what I can find."

"What's your boyfriend's involvement with Dalton?"

"Fiancé. And he's not involved with Dalton."

"He had dinner with him."

"Look, Dalton has a lot of influence in this town. He has the ear of the city council. You can't get anything done without their approval. Want a permit to renovate a house? You need approval. I told you, lot of politics in this town."

Her phone buzzed with a call. She pulled it from her pocket and looked at the display. She showed me the caller ID before answering. It was Sutton Eldridge. She swiped the screen and took the call. "What can I do for you?"

"You have a moment to talk?" Sutton asked.

"Absolutely."

28

"I'm watching that son-of-a-bitch lie on television," Sutton grumbled. "Are you watching his press conference?"

"Which son-of-a-bitch are we talking about?" Dakota asked.

"The one claiming he had no knowledge of the maintenance issues with the gondola. It's quite disgusting. You should get yourself in front of a television."

Dakota climbed off the snowmobile, and we hustled inside. I found the remote and clicked on the flatscreen in the living room, then flipped through the channels until we came across the press conference.

Dalton Callahan read from a prepared statement. "I am deeply saddened by this tragic event, and we intend to offer full transparency during the investigation into this matter. I can assure you that we have complied with all required maintenance schedules, and the obligation of such maintenance was contracted to a third party. Our thoughts and prayers are with the victims and their families in this desperate hour. I have set up a relief fund to cover their immediate medical costs and other associated expenses. Thank you."

Cameras flashed, and reporters shouted questions.

Dalton ignored the questions, and his attorney took over. "That's all for now."

The impromptu press conference had taken place on the front porch of Dalton's mountainside estate. He was in his mid-40s with dark hair, chiseled features, blue eyes, and a trimmed goatee.

Sutton's voice crackled through the speaker on Dakota's phone. "That asshole knew. Ember was going to expose him."

"Are you admitting to an affair with Ember?" Dakota asked.

"I'm not admitting to anything. I'm merely telling you what she was working on."

"This would have been helpful information a few days ago."

Sutton sighed. "I didn't think... I didn't..." He fumbled for words. "I didn't want to get involved," he finally admitted.

"Did Ember have any proof?"

"Yes. She had a source and documentation. Everything she needed. She was putting it all together and was going to run with the story. She'd been doing her due diligence to make sure everything was accurate and correct before she went public. Dalton is about to put the resort up for sale. He's been doing the bare minimum maintenance, and he didn't want to do anything that might disrupt a potential deal.

Recabling the lifts is an involved process. It can take a year, sometimes two, to complete. That's downtime, lost revenue, and would diminish the asking price."

"So, he was just going to pass it off to the next guy," I said.

"Exactly." Sutton paused. "I'm so glad I steered clear of that scenario."

"What do you mean?"

"Dalton was soliciting additional investors for an expansion project. He wanted to acquire more land, build more hotels, and more recreational facilities. He was trying to raise capital to do that, but it always seemed like he never had enough money. God only knows where it all goes. That place should be flush with cash. I considered it for a minute, then thought better of it. I don't particularly like Dalton, and this validates my gut instinct."

"Who was Ember's source?" Dakota asked.

"Ember would never reveal sources."

"Do you know where Ember kept her evidence?"

"Her apartment would be a good place to start."

"Do you have a key?"

He hesitated for a long moment. "Yeah."

"We'll be happy to come get it," Dakota said. "No purse or keys were found with her remains."

He hesitated again. "Where are you? I'll bring it to you. I would prefer it if you didn't stop by my house. My wife might start asking questions."

Dakota gave him the address, and we waited for him to arrive.

29

I slid the key into the slot, then twisted the handle and pushed open the door.

"We really shouldn't be doing this," Dakota said.

"We're just looking," I assured.

"Whatever we find won't be admissible. You know that."

"If we find something, we'll know it's worth trying to get a warrant. We'll just omit the part that we've already been here."

She rolled her eyes.

Ember lived in a luxury apartment complex on Spruce Court. We stepped into the foyer and made our way into the living room. Sliding glass doors opened to a balcony that offered a view of the slopes. It was a nice place. Tastefully decorated. It had a stylish gray sofa, a mid-century modern red leather chair, a large black framed mirror on the wall, and a state-of-the-art open-air kitchen with a bar counter.

The sleek modern fireplace added cozy warmth to the apartment.

We searched the unit, looking for papers and other evidence Ember may have collected. I noticed right away that there wasn't a computer, laptop, or tablet in the apartment. A large monitor was perched on the desk in the bedroom, but nothing was attached to it. Somebody had been in the apartment and taken her devices. It further convinced me that someone had shut her up before she could expose the corruption.

There was a file cabinet that contained bits of research and paperwork from previous cases. After digging through everything, we didn't come up with any maintenance reports or documents related to the gondola.

We left the apartment and started banging on neighboring doors, asking if anyone had been in or out of the apartment since Ember's demise.

Nobody recalled seeing anything.

We left the building, and I told Dakota to head to Madison's restaurant. I figured we'd stop by and check on her.

Dakota's phone buzzed along the way. "This is Sheriff Skye."

"I feel terrible about what happened," a voice crackled.

Dakota put in on speaker.

The man was on the verge of tears, and he slurred, "I tried to stop it. You gotta believe me."

"Who is this?"

He cried, "There were children on that gondola today. I heard two of them died."

"You work for the resort," Dakota surmised.

"I'm one of the maintenance engineers."

"You were the one talking to Ember."

"I had to tell somebody. I noticed something was not right. I made official reports. Nothing was done. Every year, those lifts passed inspection, and I couldn't believe it."

"Did you bring this to anyone else's attention?"

"The operations manager and Dalton. I was always told it would be taken care of. That the lines had passed inspection, and my assessment was incorrect."

I pulled out my phone and recorded the interaction. "Could you repeat that?"

He said it again.

"Did you talk directly to Dalton Callahan about this?"

"I did, and he assured me that any issues would be taken care of. Said he'd notify Alpine Sky Cable, and they would handle the evaluation and repair, if necessary."

"Tell me your name," Dakota said. "I'll be able to figure it out, anyway."

"Tom Jeffries," he sobbed. "I feel responsible. I've got blood on my hands."

"Do you have any proof to back up your claims?"

"I gave copies of my reports to Ember."

"Please tell me you kept the originals," Dakota said.

He hesitated for a moment. "Yeah, I got everything."

"Where are you now?"

"I'm at the Frontier Tavern."

"We can be there in a few minutes."

"No. I don't want to do this in public. I ain't stupid. I know what happened to Ember."

"What happened to Ember?"

"Somebody put two bullets into her. You ought to know that."

"You know who?"

"I wonder," he said, his voice full of sarcasm.

"Where are the original documents?"

"In my apartment."

"How about we meet you there?"

He hesitated for a long moment. "Okay."

"You sound like you've been drinking, Tom. How about we swing by and pick you up?"

"No. I'll take a cab."

"Where do you live?"

He gave Dakota the address.

She ended the call, and we drove over to the Elk Terrace Apartments. We parked on the street, hustled into the lobby, and took the elevator up to the third floor, then hustled down the hallway to unit #320. I knocked on the door, but there was no reply.

We waited outside for 15 minutes.

That turned into 20.

Then 30.

Dakota called Tom back, but he didn't pick up. It went straight to voicemail, and she left a message.

"We can always break in," I suggested innocently.

Dakota gave me a look. "If we break in, anything we acquire will be inadmissible. You know that."

"We just technically broke into Ember's apartment," I said.

"We had a key," she snarked. "We didn't technically break in. This is pushing it. We know Tom's got the evidence in this apartment. I'm not about to risk this case going up in smoke. Dalton Callahan is ultimately responsible, and I want to nail his ass to the wall."

Dakota called the station and put a BOLO out on Tom Jeffries.

We waited for another half hour, then left the building and headed across town to the Frontier Tavern. It was a couple blocks from the lifts and was popular with locals. There were flatscreens behind the oak bar, plenty of cozy booths with Chesterfield cushions, and a roaring fire crackling in the stone fireplace. There were pictures of the Old West—covered wagons, bison, hard frontier types prospecting for silver and gold.

We made our way to the bar and asked the bartender if he'd seen Tom Jeffries.

"Yeah, he left about 45 minutes ago."

"Was he driving?"

"I hope not. He came in here earlier this afternoon and started throwing them back as fast as he could. I was at the point I was going to cut him off if he didn't leave." He paused. "I called him a cab, but I don't know if he took it. It's standard procedure any time a drunk leaves the bar. I call a cab to cover my ass."

Dakota gave him a card. "If you see him in here again, give me a call."

"He in some kind of trouble?"

"No. We just need to talk to him."

"He's in here just about every day. Come back tomorrow. You'll be able to find him."

We left the bar and headed to the station. With the audio recording, Dakota filled out an application for a warrant for Dalton's arrest and one to search Tom's apartment for corroborating evidence.

By that time, the overcast sky had turned dark, and the sun had settled over the horizon, even though you couldn't see it.

We drove to Silverado to check on Madison and grab some chow. It had more of that Old West charm. Madison had done a nice job with the place.

A cute hostess greeted us with a smile. "Table for two?"

"Is Madison here?"

The pretty blonde frowned. "I'm sorry. She left for the day."

I asked Dakota if she was hungry.

"I didn't get breakfast or lunch. Plus, I owe you for last night anyway."

"This one's on me, too."

"Keep doing that, and I'll feel like I owe you something."

"You don't owe me anything."

I glanced around the restaurant and caught sight of Tara. I asked the hostess if she could seat us in Tara's section.

She smiled. "Certainly."

The hostess examined her seating chart, grabbed two menus, and led us through the maze of tables. We took a seat in a comfortable booth at the back of the restaurant, and she dealt out menus.

"Your server will be with you shortly. Enjoy your meal," she said with a smile, then spun around and returned to her post.

I called Madison to check on her. "How are you doing?"

"I'm good. I'm back at the house. I thought I could handle going to work, but I think I was doing more harm there than good. I'm just a ball of stress."

"Have you heard any more?"

"No. Why are they not responding?"

"Because they haven't planned this. They're trying to pick a location that they think is advantageous to them. They weren't planning on this. They thought that you'd roll over and transfer the funds and they would just let Amaryllis and Flynn go on the street somewhere, if they let them go at all. They're probably arguing amongst themselves trying to make a decision."

"You seem so confident."

"Just going on prior experience. This is probably the first time they've done something like this. They're not professionals."

"Is that good or bad?"

"I don't know. Amateurs are more likely to do something rash and ill-advised. Professionals don't like to take unnecessary chances. Every case is different."

"I just want this to be over. I just want my family back."

"I know. Hang in there."

"I will. JD's here. He stopped by the restaurant and rode home with me. Want to talk to him?"

"Sure."

She handed over the phone.

I caught him up to speed. "How are the guys?"

"They were snowboarding until the accident."

"Everybody's okay, right?"

"Yeah, they're fine."

"You hit the slopes?"

"No, I've been out doing my own investigation of sorts."

Tara approached the table. "Hey! Fancy seeing you here."

I told JD I'd talk to him later and ended the call.

"We thought we'd check it out," I said with a smile.

"I know I'm going to sound biased, but this really is my new favorite restaurant."

"In that case, what are your favorite dishes?"

30

"Honestly, it's a tossup between the Rocky Mountain Ravioli and the Alpine Elk Anticucho," Tara said. "The ravioli is handmade, stuffed with venison, goat cheese, and slathered with sage butter and topped with pecorino. The elk skewers are marinated in a chipotle honey glaze and served with a mountain corn salad."

"Why don't you bring us one of each to sample, and whatever my partner wants?"

"If we're splurging, how about an order of roasted quail?" Dakota said.

"An excellent choice as well."

Tara smiled and collected our menus, then darted away.

"I've worked up an appetite," Dakota said.

"I gathered."

"What do you think happened to Tom?"

"I think maybe he got cold feet and is avoiding us."

She teased, "He's clearly avoiding you."

"He doesn't know me." I sneered at her playfully. "So, did you get things sorted out with Carter?"

"Connor. Yes. I assured him that he has nothing to worry about. That you're totally not my type, and I have no interest in you whatsoever."

"So you lied," I teased.

"I didn't lie. I just omitted the part about our previous involvement. He doesn't need to be any more suspicious than he already is. There's no reason for it. We're just working a case together."

"Two cases."

"Three cases, if you count the gondola, but that's looking like it's tied into the Ember Hayes case."

We chatted for a bit, and Tara brought our salads, then our entrées. She had good taste. The food didn't disappoint. I didn't expect anything less from Madison.

Everything in the restaurant was top-notch. I had no doubt it would be a huge success. It had only been open a short time, and the place was already packed. It had gotten a good write-up in the local paper.

We were about halfway through the meal when I saw Tara get into an argument with another young man. He had pulled her aside near the hallway that led to the restrooms. He told her something that made her face contort in unimaginable ways. She looked mortified, and tears streamed from her baby blues. She hit the guy in the chest, then stormed down the hallway to the restroom.

He marched out the door.

I excused myself and strolled across the restaurant and waited for Tara to emerge from the restroom.

Her sobs filtered into the hallway.

She was in there for a good 10 minutes before coming out. Her eyes were red and puffy, and her mascara was smeared. She had done her best to put herself back together, but she looked a mess.

"Is everything okay?"

She nodded, still flustered.

"What was that about?"

"What was what about?"

I gave her a look.

"Nothing. Personal drama. I'm fine." She tried to hold it together, but her eyes misted again.

She wasn't fine.

"You can talk to me. Tell me what's wrong?"

"It's not a big deal. My boyfriend broke up with me. That's all."

"That was your boyfriend."

"No. Just the messenger."

I lifted a surprised brow. "Your boyfriend sent his friend to come in here and tell you that it was over? He didn't have the balls to do it himself?"

"Yeah, pretty much."

"Doesn't sound like you lost out on much."

She tried to agree with me, but it was still painful. Her face tensed again, and her eyes filled. She spun around and ran back into the bathroom.

I returned to the table.

"What was that about?" Dakota asked.

"Girl drama, I think." I told her the situation. "You know the guy she was talking to?"

"I think that was her brother."

"She's dating one of her brother's friends?"

She shrugged. "I can't keep up."

I sent a text to Isabella. [Can you look at the call logs for Tara Preston?]

She texted back. *[I already looked into her. She's clean.]*

[Do me a favor, keep tabs on her texts and phone calls. It's probably nothing. But better safe than sorry.]

Dakota and I finished the meal. Tara never came back to our table.

Another waitress approached. "I'm so sorry. Tara had an emergency and had to leave. I'm Celena. I'll be taking over your table. Can I get you anything else?"

We ordered dessert and coffee. After we put that away, I asked Celena for the check.

"There is no check," she said with a smile. "It's on the house."

I dug into my pocket, pulled out a fat wad of cash, and left a nice tip on the table for her.

We left the restaurant and stepped outside, only to be greeted by Connor.

"Two nights in a row? This is starting to look personal, not professional."

31

D akota huffed and glared at Connor. "Are you following me around?"

"No, but maybe I should."

"We're working a case," she said.

"It doesn't look like you're working at all."

Dakota glared at him. "Do you have any idea what's going on? You're aware of what happened on the mountain today?"

"I've seen the news."

"Connor, we'll talk about this later. I'm gonna take the deputy home, and I'll see you back at your place."

"I can find my own way home," I said. "It's not a problem."

"It's becoming a problem," Connor said, glowering at me.

His body tensed, and his hands clenched into fists. He tried to put on a good front, but this was a losing proposition for him. I think he figured that out pretty quick.

"Look, there's nothing going on here," I said. "Don't get the wrong impression of things."

"Sure looks funny to me." He squared off.

"Connor, quit making an ass out of yourself," Dakota said.

"You think I'm making an ass of myself? You're the one who's making me look like an ass. It's embarrassing. I don't like having to explain to people why my fiancée is having dinner with another man on multiple occasions, spending her days with him."

"Connor, I'm gonna tell you one more time. We are not doing this here."

"Well, maybe we shouldn't do this at all."

He gave us both another angry look, then stormed off.

Dakota called after him, "Connor!"

He kept walking.

An exasperated breath escaped her lips, and she said to me, "I'm sorry about that."

"Stop apologizing for other people. Go! Patch this up. I'll catch a ride home."

"No. He doesn't get to act like an asshole, then have me chase after him. I'm not rewarding bad behavior."

I laughed.

"Come on. I'll give you a lift."

We walked back to the patrol car and hopped in. We headed back up the mountain, winding our way up Driftwood. My phone buzzed with a call from Isabella. "I think your instincts were right on this one."

"What have you got?"

"Tara made a phone call from her cell to a prepaid device."

She had my curiosity.

"I'm not going to say there aren't legitimate reasons for using a prepaid cellular. But it always makes me a little suspicious."

"She said she just broke up with her boyfriend."

"Maybe her boyfriend is a deadbeat that doesn't pay his cell phone bill. But, if that's the case, he's got a pretty nice place on the mountain. And according to the GPS data on her phone, it looks like Tara's headed there right now."

"Maybe her boyfriend lives with his parents, and his parents are loaded."

"That's a possibility. I looked into it. The home is owned by Lawrence Highcastle. He doesn't have any kids. It looks like the property is largely used as a vacation rental."

"You did a lot of digging."

"It's what I do. Thank me later. Or you can thank me now."

"Thank you."

She gave me the address, and I ended the call.

"Do you have a lead you want to track down?" Dakota asked, having listened to my conversation.

"It's probably nothing."

"Why take the chance?"

"How about we run up the mountain and do a quick knock and talk? Then you can go work things out with your fiancé."

"According to him, he's not my fiancé anymore."

"An off-the-cuff statement made in the heat of anger," I said.

She spun the vehicle around, headed back down Driftwood, then took Alpine Pass out of town to Crystal Canyon Road. We headed up the mountain and ended up at a secluded cabin with a private drive that was ensconced by tall evergreens and plenty of acreage. Tara's silver SUV was parked in the driveway along with another vehicle—a gray SUV with Texas plates.

We pulled in behind Tara's car, and Dakota killed the engine. She called in the plates on the gray SUV.

The car came back clean.

We hopped out and strolled to the front porch of the rustic estate that had a log cabin aesthetic. We climbed the steps to the front porch, and I banged on the door.

The air was crisp and cool. Fresh snow covered the ground.

Footsteps shuffled inside, and a muffled exchange took place. Tara answered the door a moment later with surprised eyes. "What are you guys doing here?"

"We just happened to be in the neighborhood and thought we'd stop by," I said.

Her brow knitted with confusion.

"Whose house is this?" I asked.

She stammered. "It's my boyfriend's. We're trying to work things out."

"Is your boyfriend Lawrence Highcastle?"

Her face crinkled again.

"He's the owner of the house," I explained. "It's my understanding this is a vacation rental."

"My boyfriend's renting it."

"Your boyfriend must do pretty well," I said.

"He does."

"That's great. What does he do for a living?"

Her face tensed again. "What's with all the questions?"

"Oh, I don't know. I just find it a little odd that you called your boyfriend on a burner phone, and he happens to live in a vacation rental."

"This is really not a good time. Can we talk about this later?"

"No, I think now is a really good time," I said.

Movement in my periphery caught my attention. I looked to the corner of the house and saw an AR-15 angling around the corner at me, wielded by a masked thug.

"Hands in the air! Now!"

I hesitated for a moment.

"Do as I say, or the kid gets it."

32

T he masked thug with the rifle made a compelling argument. I raised my hands in the air, and he told Tara to take our weapons.

She did.

The thug moved from the corner of the house, keeping the weapon aimed at us.

He was about 6'2" and a little tubby. Built like a lineman. He had tattoos across his knuckles.

He marched us inside, keeping his distance as he forced us into the living room where another masked thug waited. I noticed the bloodstains on the carpet right away, and my heart leaped into my throat.

The perp in the living room was maybe 5'10", 165 pounds. He had the same size build as the guy that talked to Tara at the restaurant. He wore the same clothes.

In the living room, Tubby demanded that we both get on the floor.

We did, and his accomplice tied our wrists and ankles. He patted us both down to make sure we didn't have any additional weapons.

I kept staring at the crusted bloodstain on the rug, wondering what happened.

Tubby growled at Tara. "You led them straight here."

"I didn't lead them anywhere."

"Then how did they get here?"

"I don't know," Tara said.

"I want to see Amaryllis and Flynn," I demanded. "Now!"

"Shut up," Tubby said.

"What are you going to do with them?" Tara asked, her eyes flicking at us.

"What we have to do," Tubby said in a grave voice. "They've seen your face. They know who you are. You got us into this mess."

"No, you got us into this mess when you killed Flynn!" Tara cried.

My heart sank.

"I had no choice," Tubby replied. "Your boyfriend became unreasonable."

Tara clenched her teeth, and her cheeks flushed as she glared at him.

It was all starting to make sense now. This was an inside job. Flynn was having an affair with Tara and had kidnapped himself. He was using Amaryllis as a tool to extort money from Madison. He hired these fools to play the bad guys, and they took the role too seriously.

"I contacted dispatch before we came here," Dakota said. "Someone will come looking."

"By the time they come looking, we won't be here," Tubby said. He hovered over me. "You talk tough on the phone, but you don't look so tough now."

"You idiots screwed everything up," Tara said, tears streaming down her cheeks.

"I didn't screw anything up," Tubby said. "I had it all under control."

She glared at him. "I hate you!"

Amaryllis's cries filtered from a nearby room. A wave of relief washed over me. She was still alive.

Tara stepped in her direction toward the bedroom door.

"What are you doing?" the other thug asked.

"I'm going to see what's wrong," Tara replied.

"Nothing's wrong," Tubby said. "She's crying. Kids cry."

Tara ignored him and stepped toward the bedroom.

"Put on a mask," the other thug said.

"What difference does it make now?"

"Do you want her to meet the same fate as these two?"

She snarled at him. "No, Cody. I don't."

"Oh, for fuck sake." Cody had a fit. "Are you that fucking stupid? No names."

"Not as stupid as you two."

"You should never have come here," Tubby said.

Tara flipped him off, then grabbed a ski mask from the kitchen table, pulled it over her head, and stepped into the bedroom.

I figured they had been getting up-to-the-minute information about our investigation from Tara this whole time.

"What are we going to do?" Cody asked.

"Let's get Flynn and bring him inside."

The two goons hustled out the front door.

I exchanged a glance with Dakota as we struggled with our bonds on the floor.

"You wouldn't happen to have a knife handy, would you?" I asked.

"They took it."

Cody and Tubby carried Flynn's body back inside. They had buried him in a snow drift behind the cabin. Flakes of snow and ice coated the body. He was frozen stiff. The gunshot wound to the chest told me exactly how he died.

I wasn't totally sure about the *why* of it, but I figured Tubby had designs on keeping all the ransom for himself. I'm sure Flynn had concocted the idea and brought these two on for a percentage. I'm sure, as things went along, that percentage got higher and higher. People tend to reevaluate their situation once they fully realize the risks involved.

"Get some gasoline," Tubby commanded.

Cody hustled back outside.

Tubby knocked on the bedroom door. "We're leaving. Get the girl and let's go."

It was obvious where this was going. It was about to get a whole lot hotter in here. Spending a few days in the cabin, they had left trace evidence and DNA all over the place. The easiest way to get rid of it was to burn it down with us inside. A bonus.

Cody returned a few minutes later with a small can of charcoal starter.

"I said gasoline," Tubby barked.

"This was all I could find. I didn't think we were going to set the place on fire tonight."

Tubby groaned with frustration. He marched across the room, snatched the squeeze bottle of charcoal starter, and doused the couch. He sprayed the walls and tried to maximize the accelerant.

When the container was empty, he tossed it aside, then banged on the bedroom door. "Hurry up!"

Tara emerged a moment later with Amaryllis on her hip. The terrified girl cried, tears streaming down her face contorted.

It tore me up inside.

Tubby hustled them out of the house, and Cody followed. Tubby returned with a cheap disposable lighter. He set fire to the sofa and lit some of the starter that he had drizzled on the wood plank walls.

The amber flame, with a slightly bluish tint, spread along the path of the fluid, and the sharp smell of starter wafted through the air.

It didn't take long for the couch to go up in flames—a crackling inferno spewing toxic black smoke to the ceiling in ripples and waves.

So much for fire retardant fabric.

The stench of the polyurethane seat cushions contributed to the noxious smell.

"Have a nice evening," Tubby said as he hustled out of the cabin, the heat growing intense.

33

H ogtied, Dakota and I did our best to scoot away from the couch and toward each other.

Back to back, I got myself in a position to work on her restraints.

The knots were tied tight.

Every second, the flames grew hotter and expanded. Smoke collected around the ceiling, and the flames popped and crackled. It wouldn't be long before we were thoroughly roasted, but we would probably die of smoke inhalation or asphyxiation first. But not before excruciating pain.

Plastics, PVCs, and polyurethane can emit hydrogen cyanide with incomplete combustion. Cyanide binds to hemoglobin and inhibits cellular respiration. It's a double whammy. Combined with carbon monoxide, the air becomes deadly in a hurry.

I frantically worked on the rope around her wrists and finally got enough slack for her to slip free.

Dakota returned the favor, then we both worked on the ropes around our ankles while scooting away from the flames that expanded faster than I had hoped.

Within a few moments, we were both mobile. We stayed low to avoid the smoke and scurried toward the back door. We pushed out onto the deck, coughing and hacking, trying to suck in breaths of the crisp, cold air.

We hustled down the steps into the snow and trudged around the property to the front of the house, making our way back to Dakota's patrol car. By that time, flames engulfed the house and lit up the whole area, flickering the evergreens and aspens.

We climbed into the vehicle. She started up the engine and backed away from the inferno.

The other vehicles were gone.

Dakota radioed dispatch and informed them of the situation. She put a BOLO out on their vehicles.

The kidnappers had a good head start on us. No way we could catch up to them. We waited for emergency responders to arrive. The fire department had an uphill battle on its hands.

Flames soared into the sky.

EMTs treated us for smoke inhalation and gave us high-flow oxygen.

"How are you feeling?" an EMT asked. "Any dizziness, nausea, vomiting?"

"No," I replied, my voice muffled by the mask.

They were all symptoms of carbon monoxide poisoning.

Luckily, we avoided thermal burns to our airways. We were able to get out in time. Swelling can occlude passageways, and intubation is necessary. Sometimes it can continue swelling and prevent the insertion of an endotracheal tube.

The EMTs exhumed our breathing with stethoscopes. There was no wheezing or vibration.

The fire department eventually got the blaze under control.

Pierce Everett and his news crew were on the scene to soak up the dramatic visuals.

Dakota ran background on Cody. She looked at his prior arrests. He had gotten picked up on a DUI and was arrested for possession along with Huck Wilkison. From the screen in her patrol car, we looked at their mugshots and other photos. I recognized the tattoo on Huck's knuckles.

Love, Hate.

It was common practice to photograph tattoos and other identifiable marks during processing after an arrest. It was like branding yourself, and it didn't make much sense if you were involved in criminal activities. But then again, most people think they're never going to get caught.

I called Isabella and asked her to track Tara's cell phone, along with the burner she had called. Then I had to make a difficult call to Madison.

34

I wasn't sure what we'd find.

Isabella had tracked Tara's phone to Willow Creek Road. I couldn't imagine she'd be foolish enough to leave the device on, but then again, none of them were mental giants.

Her silver SUV was on the side of the road, the engine still idling, plumes of exhaust billowing from the tailpipe. The headlights illuminated the shoulder and the snow along the road. It was a secluded area shrouded by tall evergreens.

We pulled behind the vehicle, reds and blues flashing.

Two deputies in another patrol car followed.

Dakota spotlit Tara's vehicle with the side light. She had a backup pistol in the car, and I took her tactical pistol grip shotgun. We hopped out and approached the vehicle with caution.

I advanced along the passenger side.

Crimson blood stained the passenger window.

The vehicle's headlights illuminated a body lying in the snow a few feet ahead.

It was Cody.

Inside the SUV, Tara lay slumped at the wheel.

I figured Tubby was trying to get rid of anyone who could connect him to the crime. Cody and Tara had become liabilities. They had pulled to the side of the road, probably under the auspices of planning their next move. Huck took care of both of them. I don't think he realized we had already figured out his identity.

A dreadful sensation twisted my stomach.

Amaryllis was out there with a pure psychopath, and I had no idea where he was headed. Isabella hadn't been able to track his burner phone.

Dakota contacted the medical examiner, and deputies took over at the scene. We headed back to the station and filled out an application for a warrant to search the perps' apartments.

It didn't take long for the judge to sign off.

Dakota sent units to Cody's and Tara's apartments. We decided to investigate Tubby's place. He needed a place to go, and he might return to his apartment with Amaryllis. He lived in Cedar Springs. Another patrol unit followed us to his residence.

Huck lived in a three-story gray building that was U-shaped and had a small open courtyard. No gated parking or entry.

We took the switchback staircase up to the third flood and gathered outside his door. Dakota pounded a heavy fist. "Alpine County! We have a warrant."

I didn't even wait for a response. I heaved a battering ram against the door, and the jam splintered. Shards of wood scattered, and the door flung wide.

Dakota and the deputies marched inside, weapons drawn. I tossed the battering ram to the ground and followed behind with the shotgun.

It was a small, one-bedroom apartment with a tiny balcony that offered a view of the neighboring complex and the mountains beyond.

We cleared the living room and the bedroom but didn't find the perp or Amaryllis. We confiscated a laptop and a tablet. Maybe he had exchanged emails with one of the other perpetrators about their plans.

The commotion in the middle of the night drew the attention of neighbors. Curious faces poked their heads out of their apartments and gawked.

We asked if anyone had seen Huck, but nobody had. Dakota passed out cards and told them to get in contact the minute they saw the fugitive.

She told the deputies to keep watch on the apartment in case Tubby returned. We headed back to Alpine Park feeling defeated.

"We'll find him," Dakota assured on the drive.

"Let's just hope we find him before it's too late," I said.

Dakota's phone buzzed with a call. She looked at the screen, then decided not to answer. I didn't need to ask who it was. He'd been calling all night. He called back every few minutes.

She finally answered. "We'll talk when I get home."

"Where are you? Are you with him?"

"I told you we'll talk when I get home."

"What are you doing?"

"I'm driving back from Cedar Springs."

"What are you doing there?"

"Hunting a kidnapper. Now, if you don't mind, I really don't have the bandwidth for this conversation right now."

Dakota ended the call.

He buzzed back, and she didn't pick up.

"He's a little…"

She gave me a look, and I shut up.

She drove me to Madison's house and dropped me off. "I'll call if I hear anything."

"Likewise."

I hustled inside and joined Madison and JD.

She darted to me with terrified eyes. "Please tell me you've got Amaryllis."

35

Madison tried to hold it together, but she broke down into tears and started smacking my chest in anger. "You told me you'd get her back!"

"He can't run for long," I said. "He'll slip up, and when he does, we'll get him."

"You said that before, and now Flynn is dead."

"Flynn is the reason this happened."

She was still trying to process the whole thing, but it was hard to accept. Flynn had been having an affair with Tara for who knows how long.

Madison drifted to the couch and melted down, sobbing uncontrollably.

A phone call snapped her out of it. She looked at the display —an unknown caller. She answered in a shaky voice. "Hello?"

"If you want to see Amaryllis alive again, you'll transfer the money now!"

"Not until I see my daughter," Madison growled.

"Lady, I've killed three people today. A fourth isn't going to make a difference to me."

Madison's face went pale.

My phone buzzed with a text from Isabella.

I stepped away and took the call. In his frantic state, Huck had made the call straight from his burner phone. Unlike the other calls, which were routed through VoIP proxies on the dark web, this call was traceable. "He's at the Falcon Ridge Mine."

"Let me know if that phone moves," I whispered.

"Will do."

I ended the call and stepped back to Madison.

"Half now and half when you release Amaryllis," Madison said, trying to negotiate.

"All of it now, or she dies!" Huck growled.

Madison swallowed hard. "Okay. I'll transfer the money. But I swear to God, if you hurt her, you're a dead man."

Madison launched her crypto wallet and completed the transaction. She'd had it ready and waiting.

It could take minutes or hours, depending on the network volume.

"It's sent," Madison said. Hope filled her eyes, but that hope was crushed.

"I'll release your daughter when I'm safely out of the country."

Huck ended the call.

Madison's face went pale with despair. It was a punch to the gut. She stared hopelessly into space.

"We know where he is," I said. "But he might not stay there for long."

"Just get her back," she said, still staring into the distance.

She was beyond numb.

JD and I hustled out of the house, hopped into my rental, and tore out of the driveway.

"You got an extra pistol?" I asked.

JD grinned. "You know I do."

He dug into a coat pocket and displayed the weapon with pride.

I called Dakota and told her we knew where Huck was. "We are on our way there now."

"That's on private property. I'll need a warrant. How do you know he's there?"

I told her.

"No way I can get a warrant on an illegal trace. That property is owned by a corporation out of California. It's not like I can get an answer from the owner tonight."

"No warrant necessary," I said. "We're handling this."

A resigned sigh escaped her lips. "You know where you're going?"

"Not really, but JD's got it on the map."

Dakota gave me directions. "I'll meet you there. Do not move on the suspect without me."

I agreed, but I didn't know if I could hold to that promise.

The old silver mine at Falcon Ridge wasn't that far as the crow flies, but we had to drive down Alpine Pass, then around the mountain to Stag's Hollow Canyon. It wasn't like you could drive right up to the site. The area was fenced in, and it required a hike of a few miles to get to the old camp-site. It was nestled in the shadows of the ghost town of Sidewinder.

I hoped we'd get there before Huck moved on.

36

JD and I crunched through the snow, the frozen chill of winter sweeping through the evergreens. Snow fell, covering the ground with fresh powder.

We had pulled off the road, hopped the fence, and trekked toward the old mining camp. We weaved through dense spruces and aspens, stepping over fallen branches and trees.

Serrated peaks loomed. A dilapidated trestle bridge crossed Stag's Hollow Creek, leading to the abandoned site. Rusted and weathered shacks and equipment dotted the property. Some of the structures were relatively intact, while others were rusted-out shells of their former selves, missing roofs and walls. Some were built from corrugated metal, and others were made of brick. There was an old power station that had supplied electricity to the mines. In its later years, the mine had shifted from silver and gold to zinc and other minerals. Tanks of toxic PCBs remained behind, in desperate need of cleanup and remediation. An abandoned railway led into the camp, and dilapidated log retaining walls supported the trestle.

JD and I held up at the tree line across the creek.

I was surprised at how little graffiti was tagged on the walls of the buildings. Then again, it took a concerted effort to get here. This wasn't some place that you ventured to on a whim with a can of spray paint.

Huck had built a small fire in the old pump station, and the amber glow flickered through the broken windows and the gaps in the brickwork.

We took our life in our hands, crossing the creek on a small wooden bridge. I took cautious steps, my boots crunching on the snow, the boards slightly creaking, the whole bridge swaying.

Once on the other side, we advanced to the pump station and held up outside.

I peered through a window frame and saw a small fire made from kindling. The branches popped and hissed. The smoke escaped through a hole in the roof.

The interior was filled with heavy machinery with peeling green paint and bubbling rust. The floor was littered with debris. The flickering flames painted shifting shadows on the walls.

I didn't see Huck or Amaryllis anywhere.

Gunshots erupted, streaking across the campsite, pelting the brick wall beside us. Chips of debris scattered.

JD and I scampered for cover.

Huck was about 50 yards away by the old power station. He'd been scavenging wood logs around the campsite to fuel the fire. They hit the ground before the first shot.

He blasted off a few more, and muzzle flash flickered in the night. Huck took off running, and JD and I gave chase.

He ran down the dirt road, then sprinted across the old wooden bridge. It creaked and groaned, rumbling with each step.

A few boards disintegrated beneath his feet, and he fell through.

It happened in slow motion.

Huck's eyes rounded, and he tried to grasp another board on his way down.

One last attempt at salvation.

But the dry-rotted board snapped. The crack echoed through the valley, and Huck plummeted below.

It was about a 30-foot drop.

Huck landed flat on his back on top of a rock formation. The crack of his vertebrae was louder than the wood that snapped.

The air rushed from his lungs with a horrid groan.

JD and I raced toward the ravine and cautiously made our way down to where Huck lay.

He couldn't move, and blood bubbled from his mouth as his dazed eyes stared toward the dilapidated bridge above. He'd smacked the back of his head as well, and blood oozed from his scalp.

"Where's Amaryllis?" I demanded.

37

H uck gurgled something unintelligible before he died.

My jaw clenched, and I may have shouted a few obscenities that echoed through the valley.

I felt for a pulse in his neck, but he was gone.

I searched his pockets for his phone. I found two. A burner and his regular phone. The one in his back pocket had a screen webbed with cracks from the fall.

I powered it up.

It still functioned. I wasn't sure if facial recognition would work in his present condition, but the phone unlocked when I held it in front of his face. This was his personal phone. I searched the recent calls and texts, but he had deleted everything.

I thumbed through his apps and launched his crypto wallet. He had enabled biometric authentication, so I used the same facial recognition trick to access the wallet. The last transaction was the transfer of $15 million in cryptocurrencies from Madison. With a few clicks, I sent the funds back to her wallet. She would get her money back, minus the transfer fees. The money was of little consolation without Amaryllis.

I thumbed through Huck's burner, looking for any calls or text messages to accomplices, but there was nothing. I had to hand it to him—he was good about erasing digital evidence.

I texted Isabella and asked her to track the history of both phones.

JD and I climbed up the ravine and searched every inch of the campsite, looking for Amaryllis. We looked in the powerhouse, the pump station, and in all the skeletal structures. We explored every nook and cranny, then ventured into the open mineshaft. I was surprised it wasn't sealed, but you could freely walk inside.

My flashlight illuminated the way as we crept into the dank air. Rotten wood and debris littered the ground as we stepped deeper into the cave carved from solid rock. That sick sensation sat heavy in my stomach. I didn't even want to consider the unthinkable.

What if Huck had already killed Amaryllis and dumped her body somewhere?

It was a dreadful thought.

What if she was at the bottom of a mine shaft?

I treaded as far as I dared. The old wooden steps that led deeper into the abyss were fraught with danger. One wrong move, and you could find yourself at the bottom of a shaft. I didn't want to meet the same fate as Huck.

We backed out of the mine and called Dakota. I updated her on the situation and got an earful as we waited for first responders to arrive.

The sky lightened as dawn approached. Deputies swarmed, and they searched with canines. EMTs arrived, and the medical examiner hovered over Huck's remains.

I got another tongue-lashing from Dakota. She barked with fire in her eyes. "What part of *do not move on the suspect* did you not understand?"

"We were just doing a little recon when he opened fire," I said.

"You two were trespassing, and now we have a dead suspect and no idea where your niece is."

"Exigent circumstances," I defended. "We had reasonable suspicion to believe the suspect was on the property and my niece was in imminent danger."

"And what gave you that reasonable suspicion?" she asked, knowing how it was obtained.

I frowned at her.

"I'm going to take a lot of heat on this. You're lucky Pierce hasn't shown up with his news crew."

"Speak of the devil," JD muttered.

The reporter had arrived with a cameraman and a sound guy. They were on the other side of the creek and started filming the chaos.

"Go home," Dakota said. "Get some rest. I'll handle this. I think it's time we bring in the FBI and expand the search."

I agreed.

"Do not say a word to that vulture."

"Trust me, I won't."

We left the campsite and made our way across the creek, stepping on large boulders to cross the water. Neither of us were going near the bridge. We climbed up the ravine, and Pierce accosted us with his camera crew.

"Deputy Wild, can you tell us what took place here this evening?"

"No, I can't," I said, continuing past the lens.

JD and I trudged into the forest and made our way down a trail in the snow that had been worn from all the recent foot traffic.

"What are you going to tell Madison?" JD asked.

I cringed. It was going to be a painful conversation.

38

"You promised me you'd get her back!" Madison snarled. A mix of fury and sadness filled her eyes. She trembled, and she looked like she was going to hit me.

"We'll find her," I assured. "Maybe Huck had an accomplice that we don't know about."

"Or maybe she's dead in a snowdrift."

Tears filled her eyes and spilled over, streaming down her cheeks.

"Don't go there."

"It's the truth. Face it. She's gone!"

Madison took a seat on the couch, and her head fell in her hands as she broke down into sobs.

There was nothing I could say or do to fix the situation.

"I wish I never called you. I knew this was a mistake. I should have paid them right away."

"You paid him, and he still didn't give her back."

She glared at me. "Don't you dare. This could have been different if I just agreed to their demands upfront."

"You don't know that."

"Get out!" she said in a low growl that bordered on demonic.

"Madison..."

"Get. Out. I never want to see you again."

"Madison. I'm sorry."

She glared at me, the devil in her eyes.

I surrendered, backed out of the room, and gathered my belongings. There was no talking to her at this point, and I couldn't blame her.

I left with JD and drove to the Coyote Creek Lodge.

"Well, that went a little better than I expected," JD said in a dry tone.

I gave him a look.

"I was fully expecting her to shoot you."

"She doesn't have a gun."

"Thank God for small miracles."

"I messed up," I admitted.

"You did your best."

"It wasn't good enough."

"It's not over yet."

I appreciated his optimism, but we both knew it wasn't looking good.

Isabella responded. *[Huck's burner phone went off the grid when he left the cabin. It popped back up when he called Madison from the mine, then went dark again. I've got nothing in between.]*

The news was deflating.

I parked by the entrance and grabbed my roller case from the cargo area. I pulled it inside and stepped into the foyer of the palatial accommodations. I handed the keys to the valet who greeted me at the door.

At one point in time, the Lodge had been a private residence. Now it was an exclusive bed-and-breakfast with ski-in ski-out access, an indoor pool, an outdoor pool, an in-house chef, laundry service, and a complimentary chauffeur.

The Lodge was four stories of opulence. A frosted crystal chandelier hung from the ceiling in the vaulted foyer. The entrance to the estate was on level II. Below was the pool, kitchen, dining area, and garage access.

It had once been owned by a former gold medalist, Winter Van Dorn. Her father had practically owned half the mountain before he sold most of it.

JD escorted me to his guest room, and I made myself at home on the fold-out sofa bed.

The room had floor-to-ceiling window walls, a balcony that offered a view of the slopes, and elegant, mid-century modern furniture with onyx countertops and brushed nickel fixtures. It was the kind of place you could get used to real quick—except when the bill came due. The last time we stayed here, it was on the house. This time, JD was picking up the tab.

"Don't worry. Eventually, she'll realize you did everything you could do."

"I don't think that will change her opinion."

It had been a long night, and I needed to get some sleep. The fold-out bed was pretty comfortable, and I managed to get more than a few hours.

It was the early afternoon when I peeled my eyes open again. My phone buzzed with a call from Dakota.

In a desperate voice, I said, "Please tell me you found her."

39

"Tom Jeffries was found dead in his car in an alley off Smuggler's Way," Dakota said. "Looks like he's been there for a day. He never made it back to his apartment."

"Cause of death?"

"He shot himself."

I winced. "Are we sure he shot himself?"

"Do you want to come down here and see for yourself?"

"Yeah. I'd like to take a look at the scene."

"I figured you would."

I pulled myself out of bed, got dressed, then caught a rideshare to the scene with JD.

Red and blue lights flickered, and deputies kept onlookers at bay. The silver sedan was covered in snow from a heavy fall the night before. The windows were frosted. It was hard to see inside, and it was no wonder Tom hadn't been found for quite some time.

Somebody had reported the vehicle illegally parked, and when a wrecker driver came to tow it away, he found the remains.

A deputy snapped photos while Sandra examined the body.

JD and I approached, and I flashed my badge to the deputy that kept onlookers away.

"I'd say the cause of death is pretty obvious," Sandra said, backing away from the corpse.

I looked in the vehicle. A black semiautomatic pistol rested in Tom's palm. He'd eaten the barrel, and the back of his skull was now all over the headliner.

It wasn't a pretty sight, but the frigid temperature had kept things from putrefying.

The blood had drained from his face and pooled in his lower extremities. There were speckles of crimson on his hand, as one would expect. I get suspicious when I see suicides without the telltale spatter.

There was nothing obvious to indicate that this had been done by anyone other than Tom.

"Maybe he felt guilty," Dakota said.

"There was no doubt he felt guilty, but why do it on the way to see us?"

"Maybe he just didn't want to face the public. Face the reality of it. His life was about to change, and he'd be made the scapegoat."

It was a lot of pressure for anyone to face.

I told the medical examiner to do a full autopsy and run blood work just to make sure.

She gave me an annoyed look. "I don't work for you."

"Just do it," Dakota said.

"I will give it a thorough evaluation," she assured.

"I say we take a look around Tom's apartment, see if we can find those maintenance reports," I said.

"We have a slight problem," Dakota said.

Her eyes flicked around, then she nodded down the alley for us to follow. She led us back to her patrol car, and we hopped inside. In a hushed tone, she said, "Judge Vaughn denied the warrant."

"What!?" I exclaimed.

"That's bullshit," JD said.

Dakota nodded. "See what I've got to deal with? Dalton plays golf with Vaughn."

"Take it to another judge."

"It won't make a difference."

"Dalton can't have the entire town in his pocket."

"He can have more than you think. I talked to the local prosecutor. He says the recording of Jeffries by itself is not enough to get a conviction. We need something solid if we're going to take Dalton down."

"We'll get it," I assured.

"We might even need a venue change."

"I say we take a look in Tom's apartment, see what's there," JD said.

Dakota gave him a look. "No warrant, remember?"

JD shrugged.

"Legal," she said. "It needs to be legal."

"We won't take anything," JD said with a smile. "Strictly recon."

"And how do you plan on getting in?"

Jack smiled again. "We have ways."

Dakota wasn't convinced.

"It's not like Tom's going to mind." Jack paused. "Tell you what. You can drop us off and wait in the car. We'll take a look around."

"We're not discussing this."

"No discussion needed."

"That's breaking and entering. That's a crime, if you hadn't noticed."

"What's the harm?"

"You can't just pick and choose which laws to follow."

JD looked confused. "We can't?"

She gave him another look.

Dakota's phone buzzed. She took it from her pocket and looked at the screen for a moment. She hesitated, then answered the call.

I didn't need to ask who it was.

"I'm in the middle of something. Can I call you back?" Dakota said in a private voice.

"You're always in the middle of something," Connor replied, his voice crackling through the speaker in her phone.

I tried not to eavesdrop, but Connor was loud.

"It comes with the job," Dakota said, growing weary of this subject.

"Have you thought about taking a break? Maybe a vacation. We could go away somewhere. Work on *us* for a change."

"We need some work, that's for sure," she replied.

"All the more reason to pick up and go."

"I can't pick up and go. You know that."

"Yes, you can. And it would be the smart thing to do."

"What do you mean, *the smart thing to do?*"

"I'm just saying. This is a delicate situation."

"What's a delicate situation?"

"Don't be stupid."

It was the wrong thing to say.

Dakota lifted an annoyed brow. Connor had crossed a line.

"Stupid?"

"I'm not trying to start a fight with you."

"Well, for not trying, you're doing a damn good job of it."

"I don't understand why you have to be so stubborn sometimes."

"And I don't know why you have to be such an asshole sometimes."

"I'm not being an asshole. I'm just saying... You are investigating powerful and influential people."

Dakota hesitated for a moment. "What are you saying?"

"I'm saying you're important to me, and I'm concerned that you might upset the apple cart."

"I plan on upsetting the apple cart. If you haven't noticed, Ember Hayes is dead, and so is a maintenance engineer that worked on the mountain."

"You've just made my point for me."

"I appreciate your concern, but I'll be just fine."

"Not if you keep doing what you're doing. And that friend of yours isn't doing you any favors either."

Her face twisted with confusion. Dakota was a smart girl. "Has somebody asked you to tell me to back off?"

He hesitated for a long moment.

It was a guilty pause.

He tried to formulate a delicate way to put it. "Let's not make this complicated. You've got other things to do besides dig up dirt on Dalton Callahan. That's all I'm saying."

"Why are you defending him?"

"I'm not defending him. I'm looking out for you."

Dakota thought about it for a moment. "Tell me you don't have money invested in the resort. Tell me you're not in business with Dalton."

Connor was silent, and his silence was an answer.

Dakota's jaw tensed, and her face flushed. "You can tell your buddy that I'm coming for him. I'm going to get the evidence I need, and I'm going to expose him for negligence and murder."

"If you keep going down this road, he's not the only one you're going to make look bad."

Dakota hesitated a moment, putting it all together. "Did... Did you know about...?"

Connor was silent again. "You need to ask yourself where your loyalties lie."

Dakota looked flabbergasted.

"I'm just trying to look out for you. You make that awfully hard sometimes."

"I'm gonna make it easy for you. You don't have to look out for me anymore. Ever." She ended the call and looked like she was about to smash the phone. She thought better of it and slipped it back into her pocket.

Her eyes misted, and it was hard to tell if the tears were from anger, sadness, or both.

She put her hand to her face and took a moment to recompose herself as a few tears spilled. She wiped them away, then took a deep breath and pulled it all together.

"I couldn't help but overhear," I said.

"I feel so entirely stupid."

"We all make bad choices from time to time."

"I don't know how I could have misread him like that."

"Sometimes we all get blindsided." I paused. "So, what do we do now?"

Dakota thought about it for a moment. "Look, there are half a dozen agencies that are investigating that crash. They're going to subpoena records and do a forensic audit of the maintenance reports. If there was negligence involved, they'll find it. It's just a matter of time."

I gave her an astonished look. "You're not going to back off this thing, are you?"

She glared at me. "I'm not backing off anything. I'm just saying..."

"You know as well as I do that Dalton has insulated himself from this. Even if they do find negligence, he's gonna pass the buck to the lift maintenance company. He's never going to be held accountable. Worst-case scenario, he files bankruptcy and goes about his life." The more I spoke, the redder my face turned. "He silenced Ember to cover up his malfeasance. We need to connect him to that crime. You can't let him walk away from something like that."

"I'm not letting anybody walk away from anything. But I think we both need to watch our backs from here on out."

"That goes with the territory."

Dakota paused for a long moment. "So, how do we connect Dalton to Ember? No way he pulled the trigger himself. It's not his style."

"I have an idea."

40

"Y ou want a story?" I said to Pierce. "I've got a story for you."

We met him at the Snowdrift Lounge on Main Street.

I gave him the back story on Dalton's negligence. I played the recording of the call with Tom Jeffries.

Pierce listened intently, his eyes filling with exhilaration. The potential of a massive scandal would be a ratings bonanza.

"And what exactly do you want me to do with this?"

"I want you to do what comes naturally," I said. "I want you to turn this into the scandal of the century."

He grinned. "I can do that."

"How long will it take you to put it together?"

"It will lead the 6 o'clock news. The story will be syndicated nationally across the country. I'll be famous, you will be heroes, and Dalton Callahan will be behind bars."

I texted him a copy of the audio file, then he darted out of the bar.

Dakota had dropped us off, then returned to the station to fill out reports. I had asked the bartender to tune the flatscreen to the local news.

I called Madison, but she wouldn't pick up. The search and rescue team was still out there, combing the area around Falcon Ridge, looking for Amaryllis.

6 o'clock rolled around, and we were glued to the screen. The first story was a recap of the gondola incident, followed by ongoing coverage of the fact that the mountain was closed. There were interviews with numerous upset vacationers whose ski trip was ruined. They wanted a full refund —plane fare and accommodations—but the resort would only refund lift tickets. Despite the tragedy, many were still willing to ride a lift up to the top of the mountain.

There was no mention of negligence. No replay of the conversation with Tom Jeffries.

There was more coverage of Amaryllis and the kidnapping. They showed footage of the search and rescue team combing the mountain for traces of her. The helicopter circled above, and canines tried to pick up her scent. The FBI had gotten involved, and the news anchor made another call for anyone who knew of her whereabouts to contact local authorities.

We watched the entire show with no mention of Tom's recording.

I was furious.

Pierce didn't answer his phone when I called.

"That spineless son-of-a-bitch," JD muttered. "Think somebody got to him?"

"Dalton Callahan wields a lot of power and influence in this city," I said with a sigh, coming to accept the grim fact. "Seems like there are a lot of people that don't want to cross him."

"The ones that do end up dead," JD muttered.

I called Isabella and asked her to track Dalton's cell phone. After a few clicks of her keyboard, she said, "Looks like he's enjoying another nice meal at the Powder Club."

I thanked her for the information and ended the call.

I said to JD, "How about we go crash the party?"

A sly grin tugged his face.

We paid the tab, left the Snowdrift, and caught a rideshare up the mountain to the exclusive restaurant.

Valets scurried about, parking expensive cars. We hopped out of the rideshare and hustled inside. I flashed my badge to the maître d' and said, "Looking for Dalton Callahan."

His face tensed, then he pointed across the restaurant to a nice table that would normally have a view of the slopes, but the lights on the mountain were off.

We marched across the restaurant, the murmur of conversation swirling, along with the smell of fine food. Ice rattled in glasses, and forks clinked against plates.

I strode right up to Dalton's table and smiled. He and his guests looked at me with confusion. Two big bodyguards closed in.

"There's something I'd like you to hear," I said.

I had the clip queued up and ready. I turned the volume up on my phone and pressed play. Tom's voice filtered out, detailing the trouble with the lift.

41

"Is that supposed to mean something to me?" Dalton asked once the playback had finished.

"Why am I not surprised that you're indifferent to the death of several people," I said.

"I'm not indifferent. I'm deeply saddened by the tragic events, and I can assure you, Deputy, that a full investigation is underway, and we will get to the bottom of this."

"You knew there was a problem, yet you ignored it."

"And where's your proof?"

"Maybe you weren't listening."

"I was listening, and what I heard were the ramblings of a drunk, suicidal man who took responsibility for the incident. He said it himself. It was his fault. And in this day and age, how can we even be certain that's the voice of Tom Jeffries? It could be digitally manipulated. Artificial Intelligence. All manner of trickery is possible these days."

He knew damn good and well that was the voice of Tom Jeffries.

"Ember Hayes was about to expose you."

He forced a smile. "Ember Hayes was an imaginative woman. I don't recall Tom Jeffries coming to me with these concerns, but I oversee a lot of aspects of the business. If he did, I'm sure I would have referred it immediately to our contractor that handles all the lift maintenance. If you want to point fingers, Deputy, I suggest that's where you look."

His response didn't surprise me.

"Now, if you'll excuse me, gentlemen, you're interrupting my evening."

This guy got under my skin.

"You know, it seems like there are a lot of people in this town that are afraid of you. But I'm not. One way or another, I'm going to connect you to Ember's death and the lift incident."

Dalton smiled. "I see Ember isn't the only one with an active imagination. I wish you all the best in your endeavors, but you're wasting your time. So much so that I think this is bordering on harassment. And last I checked, you're not the sheriff in this town. It's my understanding that you've recently been deputized. I'm sure that can be revoked. You're out of line and out of your jurisdiction."

"Jurisdiction or not, I'm going to put you behind bars."

He feigned confusion, and a smug smirk tugged his lips. "Shouldn't you be out looking for your niece, Deputy?"

I wanted to introduce him to my fist, but JD pulled me away from the table.

"Not here, not now," he muttered.

His bodyguards stared us down.

We left the restaurant, and the maître d' seemed relieved to see us go.

Dalton was right. I should be out looking for Amaryllis, but I felt helpless about the situation. There was nothing I could do. And that made his comment burn all the more.

The investigation into Dalton seemed more tangible. There were steps to follow. A path to take. Perhaps it was a coping mechanism on my part. The search for control amid the chaos.

We caught a rideshare and headed back toward the Lodge.

Crash buzzed JD's cell on the way. "Hey, what's going on?"

"Just rattling some cages."

"Uh, we're in a bit of a situation. You think you can come down here?"

Jack groaned, and we exchanged a look.

42

S ultry music pumped through massive speakers, and delightful beauties pranced the main stage in stiletto heels. It may have been freezing outside, but it was steamy inside. *Tetons* was the premier strip club in Alpine Park. It was no surprise that the guys had found their way here.

Toned bodies wiggled and undulated to the hypnotic beat, wearing barely anything at all. Beautiful bosoms bounced free, and pert assets jiggled. With the mountain closed, business was booming. There was nothing else to do besides hit the bars in town. Drooling men stuffed dollar bills in G-strings. Others got private lap dances.

We scanned the club, looking for the guys. They were at a table near the main stage. Crash waved us over.

We weaved through the tables as waitresses in tight skirts and fishnet stockings served overpriced drinks.

"Thanks for coming," Crash said as we joined them at the table, taking a seat. Their glasses were all empty, and no girls were in their laps.

JD grabbed the leather folio on the table and flipped it open to look at the bill. His eyes rounded when he did. "How in the world did you spend that much money?"

They all exchanged a sheepish glance and shrugged. "I don't know. It just happened. One thing kinda led to another," Dizzy said.

"We tried to split it on all our cards, but they got declined," Crash said, drooping his head, looking away embarrassed.

Jack examined the itemized receipt like a forensic investigator. "You guys got bottle service?"

They nodded.

"You know how much bottle service is in a place like this?"

"We do now," Dizzy said.

"And you went through three bottles?"

"Well, the girls had some drinks," Crash said.

"I don't see any girls anymore."

"The money ran out."

"I see that you charged quite a few dances," JD said.

Dizzy smiled. "Just living the dream."

"I promise we'll pay you back," Crash said.

This sentiment was genuine, but these guys didn't have two nickels to rub together, and there was no way in hell they were ever going to pay this tab off.

JD dug out his credit card, slipped it into the folio, and handed it to the waitress when she passed by the table. She gave him a doubtful glance. "Is this going to work?"

"And then some," JD said.

She tapped the card against her mobile reader and looked surprised when the transaction went through. "Impressive."

JD smiled at her.

"You need a receipt?"

"Yes, please."

She handed him her mobile device. "Enter your email address and sign."

He did.

She smiled. "Thank you, Gentlemen. Come again."

"While you're here, bring us a round," JD said, motioning between me and him. Then he pointed at the guys. "They are cut off."

She smiled again and darted away.

"Thanks, Jack," Crash said.

Dizzy and Styxx expressed their gratitude.

"Yeah, thanks, Bro," Dizzy said. "They were pissed. The bouncer said he was gonna kick our ass."

"You guys aren't rock stars in this town," he admonished.

Dizzy smiled. "Not yet."

The waitress returned with our drinks.

"Let it go," JD said, reading my grim expression. "Nothing you can do about it right now."

The guys asked about Madison and Amaryllis, and I caught them up on the details.

We enjoyed a few cocktails and took in the scenery.

Dakota called, but it was too loud in the club. I let it go to voicemail, then texted her. [What's up?]

[Did you storm into the Powder Club and confront Dalton?]

[Yup!]

[Smooth move. He called the mayor, and the mayor called me. Remember what I said about subtly?]

[I was subtle.]

[I'm taking heat for deputizing you.]

[Did you think this was going to be easy?]

[I need your Alpine County badge back.]

[What!? You're breaking up. I can't hear you.]

[Funny. I'm serious. I'll handle this from here.]

[You're not backing down, are you?]

[I'll handle it.]

I grumbled an obscenity. Perhaps I shouted it.

"What's the matter?" JD asked.

I let him read the exchange.

While he did, I glanced around the club and noticed a skinny guy a few tables over. The bracelet on his right wrist caught my eye. It glimmered in the light for an instant—an ouroboros.

It was a unique piece of jewelry. Unmistakable. It was the same as the one worn by Quentin's accomplice. The skinny guy had the same eye color and mannerisms.

It had to be him.

43

JD and I approached the perp and stood on either side of his chair. He was in the middle of a lap dance. A mesmerizing young lady jiggled her wares in his face. He didn't notice us for quite some time. Understandably so. She was quite the distraction. He finally gave us an angry scowl. "You guys got a fucking problem?"

Skinny's eyes rounded as he recognized me.

He pushed the girl off of him. She tumbled away, hit the table, and spilled his drink.

Skinny sprang from his seat and tried to dart away, but JD grabbed him and brought him to the ground. In an instant, he was face down on the grungy carpet that was home to plenty of spilled beer and whiskey.

The dancer climbed off the floor with a twisted face. "Fucking asshole!"

JD dug into his pocket and slapped cuffs on the scumbag.

We yanked him to his feet and escorted him out of the club.

The commotion drew plenty of stares, and the bouncer approached along with the manager.

I flashed my badge, and they backed off.

Dizzy and the gang watched with slack jaws.

They stayed at the table, and I hustled back to get them. "If you hadn't noticed, we're leaving now."

I escorted them out of the club, and we all spilled onto the sidewalk.

The biting wind whipped around the building. It was a sharp contrast from the cozy warm interior with young lovelies ready to stoke the flames of desire.

JD shoved the perp against the wall, and I taunted him. "I can't tell you how excited I am to see you again."

"I don't know you. What are you talking about? I didn't do nothing. Let me go."

I laughed.

"Your buddy, Quentin, is in jail. You're going to be joining him. Are you aware of the penalties for kidnapping?"

"I didn't kidnap nobody."

You broke into my sister's house and held us hostage for a night while you were looking for something in the safe. Sound familiar?"

"You got the wrong guy."

"Your bracelet tells me otherwise."

Skinny swallowed hard. "What!?"

"Little piece of advice. Next time you break into someone's home and hold them captive, don't wear any identifiable clothing or jewelry."

"Man, I don't know what you're smoking. You can get one of these bracelets anywhere. Doesn't mean shit."

"I do appreciate you, though."

Skinny's face wrinkled with confusion.

"That big guy was ready to put a bullet in me. You were hesitant. Because of that, I'm going to offer you a deal."

He remained silent for a long moment, considering his options. "What kind of deal?"

"You tell me where I can find that big bastard, and you won't spend the rest of your life in prison."

"You got nothing on me."

"You're catching me on a bad day. I'm not in the mood for any nonsense."

"Sorry, I can't help you. You're making some kind of mistake."

"You know, there are a lot of places someone like you could get lost. Places where they'd never find your body. You have to ask yourself, what kind of cop am I? Am I the kind that will cut you loose if you tell me where to find your accomplice? Or am I the kind of guy that will take you out to a mine shaft and dump you down a bottomless hole?"

Skinny swallowed hard again.

"His name is Diesel."

"Diesel?" I said with a doubtful tone.

"That's how Quentin introduced him."

"Where can we find him?"

"I don't know. I never met him before that night."

"What were you clowns after?"

He hesitated for a long moment.

44

"Quentin's dad was a collector of rare artifacts," Skinny said. "He had priceless items from around the world. All of it was accounted for and distributed in accordance with the will, except for the Diamond Lion."

"The Diamond Lion?" I asked.

"It was commissioned by some duke or prince as a wedding gift in the early 1900s. Articulated silver, white diamonds, and emerald eyes. Quite a stunning piece, from what I understand. It was stolen in the late '60s and was never seen again in legitimate circles. Quentin's dad supposedly won it in a poker game 20 years ago. It had been part of his private collection ever since. He couldn't list it in his will. It can only be sold on the black market. Still, it's worth millions."

"And you guys were going to steal it and split the proceeds," I said.

"We weren't going to steal it. It was Quentin's, to begin with."

"It wasn't Quentin's. It was his father's. And his father cut Quentin out of the will."

"You would never have missed it. You didn't even know it was there."

"It wasn't there."

Skinny frowned. "Was it really in the safe deposit box at the bank?"

I shook my head.

"I knew it."

"Where do we find Diesel?"

Skinny shrugged. "I don't know."

I called Dakota. "Hey, I need you to look for anyone with a criminal history that goes by the nickname Diesel."

"You're not a deputy in this county anymore, Tyson."

"This is the guy that broke into Madison's house and held us captive. I've got his accomplice."

"You've got his accomplice in custody?"

"He volunteered the information in exchange for a deal."

"So you kidnapped him?"

"Not technically."

"If you have him in handcuffs and are holding him against his will, that would technically be kidnapping since you're not law enforcement in this county anymore."

"Citizen's arrest."

She huffed. "What kind of a deal?"

"He walks away if his testimony leads to a conviction of both Quentin and Diesel," I said, the words aimed both at Dakota and Skinny.

"I gotta testify?"

"Yep."

Skinny cringed.

"You're not authorized to make such a deal," Dakota said.

"I'm sure you can work it out with the local prosecutors. It's a small town. You've got some pull."

"Not as much as you might think. Why are you going so easy on this guy?"

"I'd have a bullet in my head if it wasn't for him."

"Reasonable. Hang on while I look this up."

She found her way to the keyboard and tapped the keys. A moment later, she said. "Nope. Nobody in the area that goes by Diesel with a criminal history."

I asked Skinny. "How does Quentin know Diesel?"

"I think they met in the joint."

I relayed the information to Dakota. "Give me the names of everyone that was recently released from the same facility as Quentin."

She tapped the keys again. "There's a long list of names here. Thousands of people get released every year."

I asked Skinny, "How did Diesel get his name?"

Skinny shrugged. He thought about it for a moment. "I think Quentin called him Vinnie once."

I relayed the information to Dakota.

She read the names from the list. "Vincent Ross, Vincent Sparks, Vincent Drake, Vincent Simmons, Vincent Foley, Vincent Dorian, Vincent Murphy, Vincent Young, Vincent de Paul, Vincent DeSalle—"

I cut her off. "DeSalle. Diesel. Text me his mug shot."

A moment later, the image buzzed my phone. I showed it to Skinny. "Is this him?"

"Yeah, that's him."

I relayed the information to Dakota.

"Where are you?"

I mumbled, "Tetons."

"Tetons? Really?" she said in a disappointed tone.

"Long story."

"I bet." She sighed. "Don't go anywhere. I'm coming to pick up your perp."

"We'll be waiting."

I ended the call, and we loitered on the sidewalk until Dakota pulled up in her patrol unit. She climbed out and joined us. She asked Skinny his name, and he told her.

"Okay, Jeremy," Dakota said. "Tell me everything you told Deputy Wild."

He repeated the story.

"Alright, you're under arrest for breaking and entering... You have the right to remain silent..."

"He said he was gonna cut me loose," Skinny said with wide eyes.

"You don't get cut loose until we have Diesel in custody."

"Man, this is bullshit," Skinny said, shaking his head.

She stuffed him into the back of the patrol unit.

"I want my handcuffs back," JD said.

"Take mine," she said, handing them to him.

He frowned at her.

"Now, stay out of trouble, and leave this up to me. I'm going to take a statement from him and get a warrant. I'll send deputies to pick up Diesel. I'll let you know when it's done."

"We'd really like to tag along."

"You're not tagging along anywhere. You two have been drinking, and you smell like cheap perfume."

"Don't be jealous," I teased.

She stared at me. "The last thing I am is jealous."

"Any word on the search?"

Dakota frowned and shook her head. "They've walked every inch of the terrain around the mine. No trace of Amaryllis. I'm sorry. They'll pick it up again tomorrow."

"Has the mine been thoroughly searched?"

"As much as possible. The dogs didn't pick up a scent." She paused. "How's Madison holding up?"

"I don't know. She won't take my calls."

I explained the situation.

"Look, there's nothing you can do right now," Dakota said. "Go out, have fun, blow off some steam."

"How am I supposed to have fun while my niece is still out there?"

"I don't know," she said with a grim expression. "Seems like you were having fun at Tetons."

I sneered at her. "We were getting these guys out of trouble," I said, pointing to the band.

"I know you're putting a lot of pressure on yourself." She stammered, "I think you need to brace for the possibility…"

She didn't want to say it, and I didn't want to hear it.

"That's a possibility I'm not willing to accept."

"Some things are out of your control. There's nothing you can do. Don't beat yourself up over it. You did everything you could."

"It wasn't enough."

"I'm sorry," she said in a sincere tone before walking around to the driver's side. "Try to stay out of trouble."

She climbed in and drove away.

"Where to now?" Crash asked.

45

"I think you guys have exceeded your party budget," JD said.

"A minor overage," Crash assured.

JD looked at him in disbelief. "Minor?"

"This whole thing has been stressing us out. We just wanted to blow off some steam. Like the sheriff said."

JD gave him a doubtful glance.

"I'm serious. It's totally messed up. We hate that Tyson's going through this. I wish there was something we could do."

"Maybe there is," I said. "We're gonna head back to the Lodge, make up some flyers, and you're going to pass them out at every bar and restaurant in town. Plaster them on every wall, light pole, and bench in Alpine Park."

The guys nodded.

"We can do that," Crash said. "In the meantime, we'll recon optimum spots and ask around."

JD gave him a look before digging into his pocket and handing over a wad of cash. "When you guys spend this, it's gone."

Crash smiled. "Thanks, Jack."

We said our goodbyes and called for a rideshare. A few minutes later, a silver SUV pulled to the curb, and we climbed into the backseat. The driver zipped us across town and up the mountain toward the Lodge.

The headlights from the car behind us illuminated the cabin and shined bright in the rearview mirror, squinting our driver's eyes.

"Go around, asshole!" he exclaimed.

The vehicle behind us was right on our ass. There wasn't really a good place to pass on the winding road. Our driver drifted to the shoulder to give the vehicle extra room.

It swerved around, and the engine howled as it pulled alongside us, crossing the double yellows. The passenger window rolled down, and an Uzi emerged.

Muzzle flash flickered from the barrel.

Bullets pelted the glass.

Windows shattered, and debris rained down.

JD and I ducked for cover.

Bullets pinged and popped against body panels.

One of the bullets hit our driver.

Crimson blood splattered against the passenger seat and window. He slumped forward, honking the horn, veering to the right. With his foot still somewhat on the gas, we plowed off the road down a slight ravine and smacked into a tall evergreen.

The hood crumbled like an accordion.

Metal twisted and popped.

More glass shattered.

A deafening bang from the airbags filled the vehicle.

The front windshield webbed with cracks as the bag expanded.

Steam billowed from the hood, which now obstructed the forward view.

The seatbelt dug into my hips.

It took a moment after the crash to regain my wits.

The smell of oil and gasoline drifted into the cabin.

I looked at JD. "Are you okay?"

His face was beet red, and his eyes bulged, his long blonde hair was tousled.

He nodded.

The assailants had stopped on the roadway ahead. The shooter hopped out of the passenger seat and marched off the road to make sure the job was done.

I drew my pistol, angled it through the shattered window, and opened fire as he approached. I squeezed the trigger twice, and the report hammered against my palm. The barrel flashed, and the bullets zipped through the air, hitting the masked goon in his thoracic cavity.

He spun around and flopped into the snow.

His accomplice in the vehicle stomped the gas, and tires squealed.

I fired two shots at the black SUV, pelting the right rear quarter panel as it sped away into the night.

I forced my passenger door open. It was stuck and took a few shoves. It popped and clambered. The frame was bent.

More shards of glass fell into the snow from the window frame like drops of rain.

I climbed out of the vehicle and advanced to the perp.

He lay in the snow writhing and moaning. I had tagged him near the shoulder and probably severed a nerve and an artery. Blood spurted from the wound. His clavicle was probably in a million pieces.

He tried to put pressure on the cavern, but crimson still seeped between his fingers.

His Uzi had fallen into the snow, and his right arm was useless.

With his left hand, he tried to reach for a pistol in his waistband as I approached. As soon as he removed his hand from the crater, it gushed more.

"Don't move!" I shouted.

He had a choice to make.

I kicked the Uzi away.

By that time, JD had joined me. I kept my pistol aimed at the scumbag while JD knelt beside the perp and took his pistol.

"I'd keep pressure on that wound if I were you," JD said.

I pulled the ski mask from the assassin's head and recognized him right away. He was one of Dalton's security guards. The guy Dalton hired to do his dirty work. The guy he'd likely tasked with killing Ember Hayes.

I just needed to prove it.

"I'm gonna make this really easy for you," I said. "You're gonna tell me what I want to know, and I'll make sure you get the appropriate medical attention. If you don't, you could bleed out right here before emergency services arrive."

He looked up at me with round eyes, his skin growing pale.

"You're not looking so good," JD said to him.

46

EMTs and paramedics arrived. They took over and treated the scumbag. Red and blue lights flashed as patrol cars arrived on the scene.

"I see you took the whole *staying out of trouble* thing to heart," Dakota snarked as she approached. "Are you two okay?"

"I'm sure we'll be stiff and sore tomorrow," JD said.

"You recognize that guy?" I asked.

She looked past me at the perp as the EMTs attempted to stabilize him. "That's one of Dalton's guys, isn't it?"

I nodded. "When you run ballistics on his pistol, you're probably gonna find it's a match for Ember Hayes."

I played a recording I'd made of the assassin's confession:

"Who put you up to this?" I asked the perp.

The assassin's labored voice crackled through the speaker on my phone. "Who do you think?"

"Dalton?"

The scumbag didn't say anything.

"I need you to say it."

"I work for Dalton. He hires me to clean up his problems."

"We were one of those problems," I said.

"You should have walked away."

"It looks like you should have walked away. Was Ember Hayes one of his problems, too?"

He didn't say anything.

"You and I both know you were the trigger man. You're already going down for murder. Our driver's dead. You have an opportunity here to make things a little easier for yourself." In an understanding voice, I said, "You were just following orders, right?"

He remained silent.

"Time is running out. *If* you make it to a hospital, and *if* they can save you, you're gonna be looking at a long stretch. Maybe you can shorten that time by implicating your boss. Maybe you can do your time in a more comfortable location. It's all up to you. What's it going to be?"

"Look, I just do what Dalton tells me."

"And Dalton told you to kill us and Ember Hayes."

"You catch on quick. Now call 911."

"Who drove the SUV?"

He hesitated. "Xavier Pratt."

"What's your name?"

"Trevor Farrell."

I ended the recording.

Dakota's eyes narrowed at me. In a hushed voice, she said, "Did you withhold medical treatment from him?"

"No. Not at all. JD was attempting to stop the bleeding while we waited for the EMTs to arrive," I said innocently. "I may have asked him a few questions before I contacted emergency services."

"You coerced a confession under duress."

"That's for the courts to decide. I suggest we use this to get an arrest warrant for Dalton while we can. Judge Vaughn can't deny this."

She sighed and shook her head, exasperated.

Pierce and his news crew arrived on the scene. They hopped out of the van, and the cameraman shouldered his rig and started soaking up footage.

"Deputy Skye," Pierce said as he approached. "Can you—"

"No comment."

The lens focused on us.

"Deputy Wild, were you involved in the incident?"

I palmed the lens and pushed it away, glaring at the pompous reporter.

The cameraman tried to swing the lens back in my direction, but I gave him a look. He realized that continuing to film us would be taking his life in his hands. He lowered the camera, walked away, and started gathering more footage of the EMTs as they worked on the assassin.

"Thanks for airing that clip I gave you," I snarked.

Pierce tensed and took a deep breath. "Circumstances beyond my control."

"Who got to you?"

"Nobody *got* to me. I don't know if you're aware, but I don't run the network. The powers that be didn't want to put it on air. That was the end of it."

I didn't believe it for a second.

Pierce stepped away and rejoined his crew.

The EMTs got the assassin stabilized and loaded him into the meat wagon. The lights spun up, and the ambulance pulled away.

Sandra and her crew examined our driver, then bagged the remains.

"I need your weapon," Dakota said.

My face wrinkled at her.

"You know the drill. Surrender your weapon. There's gonna be a full investigation. If you were still deputized, I'd put you on administrative leave."

I frowned at her and reluctantly complied. "You're leaving me defenseless. You realize that, right? Do you really think that's the best course of action in a situation like this? Apparently, I've made quite a few enemies in this town."

"Let's at least pretend to go through the motions," she said.

"That's my pistol," JD said. "And I want it back."

"You'll get it back," Dakota assured. "Come on. I'll give you a lift back to the Lodge."

JD and I exchanged a confused look.

"Lodge? We're not going back to the Lodge. We're going with you. You're going to get a warrant, and we're going to arrest Dalton."

She laughed. "There is no *we*. I'm going to do all of that. You two are going to go back to being civilians."

"Civilians?" JD's face crinkled like he smelled something bad. I'm sure I looked the same way.

"Sit this one out. Do not argue with me."

"What about Xavier Pratt?"

"I'll handle him."

"We should look into his girlfriend."

"There's that word *we* again." She paused. "And how do you know who his girlfriend is?"

"It was on his social media profile. I looked it up while I waited for you to get here. Xavier is probably on the run. He'll need a place to go. I mean, the way I figure it, he went back to Dalton's and told him things went south. Dalton probably told him to get rid of the vehicle and lie low. If it were me, I'd ditch the car and get the hell out of town. I don't think I'd stick around, waiting for the cops to ask questions."

"That would look suspicious."

"It beats talking to the cops. I wouldn't be surprised if Dalton put him on a private jet."

Dakota sighed. "Who is his girlfriend?"

"Mandy Lake."

"I'll send a patrol unit by her place, and I'll send one to Xavier's residence. But you two are going home."

I raised my hands in surrender and sighed, "Okay. Whatever you say, boss."

She scowled at me. "I am not your boss."

"Thank God," I teased.

We hopped into her patrol car, and she drove us toward the Coyote Creek Lodge.

"I really think you're going to need an experienced tactical team to take Dalton down," I said.

"I have an experienced team," Dakota assured.

"You need us to ID the shooter's car."

"Dalton knows things went wrong. You said it yourself—he probably had Xavier ditch the car."

I shrugged.

"Did you get a look at the driver?"

"No."

"I don't see any legitimate reason to let you tag along."

"You realize you wouldn't have this information if it weren't for us," JD said.

Dakota paused. "I'm starting to have a lot of sympathy for your boss back in Coconut Key."

"We don't have a boss," JD clarified. "We're volunteers."

"He still has to put up with you, and that seems to be quite the challenge."

JD flashed a big smile. "We get results."

Dakota rolled her eyes, then sighed. After a moment of contemplation, she said, "I'm going to regret this."

I tried to contain a grin, knowing what was coming.

"I'm going to let you tag along as *observers*. That's it."

"I just want to see Dalton's face when you slap the cuffs on him," I said.

"Let's see if that recorded confession of yours is enough to get a warrant," she said in a doubtful voice.

47

D akota banged a heavy fist against Dalton's front door.

Judge Vaughn signed off on the warrant this time. It was a little too hard to ignore. At some point, the rats would jump ship. Dalton was going down.

He had a nice mansion on the mountain just off Bear Paw Lane. Surprisingly, it wasn't the biggest place in Alpine Park. It had a mid-century modern aesthetic with lots of windows and elegant stonework. There were a few expensive SUVs in the driveway—a red Mercedes AMG G 63 and a blue Lamborghini Urus.

I didn't see the black Yukon.

Dalton answered the door before deputies were willing to break it down. "Good evening, Sheriff. What can I do for you at this hour?"

"We have a warrant for your arrest," Dakota said, trying not to gloat.

He scoffed. "Excuse me?"

"You heard me. Turn around and put your hands behind your back."

"What's this about!?" he asked with a tight face.

"Two counts of conspiracy to commit murder, for starters."

"That's ridiculous."

"I'm willing to listen to your side when we get down to the station," Dakota said. "Turn around and put your hands behind your back."

He begrudgingly complied, and Dakota slapped the cuffs around his wrists. Dalton looked stunned. This kind of thing wasn't supposed to happen to him.

"You're making a career-ending decision," he warned.

"The last time I checked, the people of Alpine County have the final say on whether I have a career or not. Not you, not the mayor, not anyone else."

"Where's Xavier?" I asked.

"I let him go earlier today," Dalton said.

"You fired him?"

"Yes."

It was a convenient story.

"What for?"

"I see no need to discuss private matters."

"Do you own a black Yukon?"

"It was stolen. I'd been meaning to report it."

Dakota read him his rights and escorted him to the patrol car. She stuffed him inside, and deputies searched the house.

Dakota put a BOLO out on Xavier.

Dalton was taken to the station, processed, printed, and put into an interrogation room.

We convinced Dakota to let us sit in on the interview, but Dalton was smart enough to keep his mouth shut. The first thing he asked for was an attorney, so there wasn't much of an interview aside from a few veiled threats.

Dakota gave us a ride back to the Lodge. Jack's phone buzzed along the way. Crash's voice filtered through the speaker. "Yo, where you at?"

"We're heading back to the Lodge."

"Change of plans. You gotta come meet us."

"You're not in trouble again, are you?"

"No, we're at this killer house party on the mountain. There's a ton of free booze and plenty of babes. "

"You have my attention," JD said.

"You're never going to believe who we ran into. Chloe-C! This is her house," Crash said in awe.

Chloe-C was one of the biggest pop stars on the planet. We'd opened for her once before in NYC, and we had a bit of history.

"She's about to start another European tour, and she wants the band to open for a few shows. You and Tyson need to get here and seal the deal."

JD said to Dakota, "Change of plans."

He asked Crash for the address, then told Dakota.

"I'm not your personal taxi service."

"That's okay," Jack said. He laid it on thick. "You can drop us off here, and we'll try not to freeze to death in the cold while we call for a driver."

Dakota rolled her eyes.

She turned around and drove us to the other side of the mountain and up the hill. Cars lined the shoulder of the road a half mile away. The place was packed.

Dakota dropped us off at the entrance to the driveway.

"You want to come in?" I asked.

"Unlike you two, I need to recharge my batteries. I'm beat. Do you guys ever sleep?"

"I'll sleep when I'm dead," JD said.

He hopped out of the car, and I followed. I looked back at Dakota.

"I'll call you tomorrow," she said.

"How's things with the fiancé?"

"Ex-fiancé."

I smirked.

"Try to stay out of trouble. I mean it this time."

I closed the door, and she spun around and drove down the mountain.

Music thumped, echoing from the house. Revelers came and went. We climbed the steps and walked in through the front door. The place was thick with bodies. Beautiful women in tight leggings and sheepskin boots. An attendant checked coats, and waitstaff hustled about with hors d'oeuvres and drinks. This was a real party, and no expense had been spared.

We made our way through the vaulted foyer and stepped into the large living room. Floor-to-ceiling window walls offered a view of the patio. There was a heated pool that must have cost a fortune to keep warm in the winter. Steam rose from the Jacuzzi that was filled with magnificent lovelies in skimpy bikinis, despite the frigid air.

Everybody wanted to hobnob with celebrities, and there were a few scattered about the crowd. I recognized faces from TV and the movies. If you threw a stick, you'd hit a movie star or a pop icon in Alpine Park.

I saw more than a few people sniffling and snorting, rubbing their noses, talking incessantly with wide eyes. It's not like people were doing lines of cocaine off the glass coffee table, but there were more than a few people that made trips to the bathroom and some that didn't even bother to hide it.

We caught up with Crash and the guys in the kitchen.

"Where's Chloe?" I asked.

"She's around here somewhere," Crash said.

"How did you meet up?"

"We met these girls at the Snowdrift, and they said Chloe-C was having a party. They didn't believe us when we said we knew her, so we had to prove them wrong."

"Where are the girls now?"

Crash frowned. "They ditched us for Jackson Fisher."

He had a hit TV show, and a crowd of girls gathered around him, hanging on his every word.

Chloe descended the steps and weaved her way through the crowd. She couldn't make it two feet without somebody stopping her to congratulate her on her new album or take a selfie. She accommodated all and slowly made her way across the living room to the kitchen.

Chloe was a gorgeous blonde with a petite figure, full lips, and hypnotic eyes. She had the perfect combination of sweet and sinful.

She flashed a brilliant smile and flung her arms around me. "Oh, my God. I can't believe you're here."

"I didn't know you had a house in Alpine Park," I said.

"I just got it. What do you think? Pretty fancy, huh?"

"Moving up in the world," I said.

She was already on top.

"I saw the guys, and I was like, no way! It seems fate has brought us together."

I smiled. "It seems it has. Congratulations on the new album."

"Thank you. Number one. Not too shabby." She flashed that bright smile again.

"You deserve it."

"It's so good to see you again." Her big eyes sparkled.

"How is your boyfriend?"

"I don't have a boyfriend."

I smiled.

"I was just telling Crash you should join me on the tour for a few dates. It would be fun. Just like old times." There was a naughty glimmer in her eyes.

The last time we opened for her, Chloe and I had a little adventure beneath the stage during the show. Good times indeed.

"I'm gonna put you in touch with my manager, and you guys can hash out all the details."

"Sounds good to me."

"You still have the same number?"

"I do."

Her mouth scrunched. "I know. I've been really bad about keeping in touch. The tour, then recording, then, you know..."

"I totally get it."

"What have you been up to?" she asked.

I updated her on the current situation.

She frowned, and sadness knitted her brow. "I'm so sorry."

A woman stepped to Chloe. "I hate to interrupt, but can I pull her away for a moment?"

"Tyson, this is my new publicist, Blakely."

We smiled and exchanged pleasantries. Chloe introduced her to the rest of the band.

"They're going to be playing a few tour dates with us," Chloe said.

Blakely smiled. "Wonderful." She went back to business. I don't think she gave a rat's ass. "Listen, Max Ivy is here. He's the head of product marketing for *Pear*™. He wants to talk to you about a sponsorship deal on the tour for their new wireless earbuds."

Chloe smiled at me. "Do *not* go anywhere."

"I'll bring her right back, I promise," Blakely said.

She ushered Chloe away and weaved through the crowd.

"I like her," JD said.

Chloe had certain endearing qualities.

I watched her slip through the crowd and caught a glimpse of a big guy making an exchange with another partygoer. In an almost unnoticeable manner, cash was exchanged for a baggie of a white powdery substance. If you weren't paying attention, you'd miss the interaction.

"Is that?" I asked.

I pulled my phone from my pocket and scrolled through my photos, looking for the mug shot of Diesel.

JD studied the image. "Yep."

My jaw tightened. "Let's go get that son-of-a-bitch."

48

J D and I moved toward the big guy, pushing through the crowd.

Diesel spotted me and did a double take. His eyes rounded, and he bolted through the crowd, bowling people over as he headed toward the patio.

Drinks spilled, and faces twisted.

"Fucking asshole!" a girl shouted.

He pushed through the door and raced past the pool and the Jacuzzi.

JD and I gave chase.

He trudged through the snow and quickly found himself in knee-high powder.

JD and I barreled after him, and it didn't take long to work up a sweat. My heart punched against my chest, and my legs drove me through the fresh powder.

Chloe's place wasn't far from the slopes. Diesel hustled down an access trail.

JD and I followed.

The narrow path was lined with aspens and evergreens.

Diesel drew a pistol from his waistband and angled it over his shoulder. He opened fire, and muzzle flash flickered from the barrel.

The bullet snapped thru the air.

JD and I took cover on the side of the trail behind some trees.

Diesel kept running.

He hit the slopes and started down the mountain, weaving around moguls the size of Volkswagens. He slipped, fell, and slid down the slope a few yards before crashing into another mogul.

Diesel didn't stay down for long.

He sprang up and kept shuffling down the mountainside.

JD and I hit the slope, and Diesel fired a few haphazard shots at us.

He made his way down to a flat cross trail and blasted a few more shots at us.

We took cover behind a mogul, and plumes of powder erupted with each bullet hit.

Diesel sprinted through a valley of evergreens to a neighboring run.

JD and I followed down the cross trail.

Diesel plunged down a double diamond, kicking up powder. The mountain had been closed for two days now, and with the recent snow, the slopes were unmolested.

Diesel slipped and fell again.

We reached the run, and he sprang to his feet and blasted a few more shots at us.

We took cover as bullets snapped through the air, echoing off the mountainside.

The slope was steep and not for the faint of heart. This was an expert run. I don't know what level of ability Diesel had on the slopes with a pair of skis or a snowboard, but on foot, he wasn't exactly gonna win any points for style or grace.

He slid down the mountain, tumbled, and came to an abrupt stop when he crashed into another mogul.

He took a few more potshots at us as we hovered at the top of the ridge.

JD and I hit the snow, taking cover at the edge of the slope.

Diesel started down the mountain again.

We plunged down after him. He was pretty far away, and his aim sucked.

Diesel made it several more frantic yards before he took another tumble. This time, when he fell, the gun went off.

Pro tip: If you're going to run with a firearm, remove your finger from the trigger. It makes life a lot less painful. You pay for poor trigger discipline sooner or later.

Diesel writhed and moaned on the mountainside, the nearby powder sprayed with crimson.

JD and I cautiously made our way down the run and approached. Jack kept his weapon aimed at the scumbag.

By the time we arrived, the moaning and groaning had stopped. Diesel had bled out. The bullet clipped him in the neck and severed his carotid artery. Neck wounds are some of the worst. The bullet hit part of his mandible and fragmented.

It wasn't a pretty sight.

I knelt down and felt for a pulse as a matter of protocol, but he was long gone.

He'd been shooting at me with my own gun—the one he'd taken from me at Madison's.

I called Dakota. "Hey, remember when you said stay out of trouble? Yeah, about that..."

49

First responders swarmed, and I filled Dakota in on the situation while the medical examiner did her business. Camera flashes illuminated the moguls as a deputy chronicled the scene.

"I don't know if I should commend you two or be upset," Dakota said.

I smiled. "Well, Diesel's not gonna be invading anyone's home now."

"I suppose Alpine Park is a little safer," she admitted. "You saw him at the party?"

"Yeah. I was talking to Chloe-C. It was her party."

"I know. You mentioned."

"We go way back," I said casually.

"They dated for a minute," JD said.

"You dated Chloe-C?"

"Don't be jealous," I teased.

She scoffed. "I'm not jealous."

She was a tad jealous.

The medical examiner's team bagged the remains, and Diesel's corpse was taken down the mountain on a sled behind a snowmobile.

"Do you think you can make it through the rest of the evening without killing anyone?" Dakota asked.

"I didn't kill anyone this time."

She gave me a look. "You need a ride down the mountain, or are you going back to the party?"

JD looked at his watch. "The night is still young."

Dakota rolled her eyes.

It wasn't that young.

There wasn't enough room on her snowmobile for two people. She gave JD a ride back to the party, then came back and got me as the responders were clearing out.

I hopped on the back of the snowmobile, but Dakota headed down the slope instead of taking me back to Chloe's. "Where are we going?"

"I'm going to make sure you stay out of trouble for the rest of the night."

"How are you going to do that? Arrest me?"

"If I have to."

We headed down to the base of the mountain and dropped
the snowmobile at the substation. We climbed into her patrol
car and drove a few blocks to her apartment. She pulled into
the gated parking below the building and killed the engine.

I gave her a curious look. "What are we doing here?"

"You're under house arrest until morning."

I laughed. "I'm staying here with you?"

She climbed out of the car, and I followed through the
parking garage to the elevator. She pressed the call button,
and the doors slid open a moment later.

We stepped inside, and the doors closed. She pressed the
button for the third floor.

"I don't think this is a good idea," I said, trying to be a gentleman. "You just broke up with your fiancé. Your head's all
screwed up. You'd just be using me for sex, and I wouldn't—
"

"Shut up," she said, crashing into me. She lifted onto her
tiptoes and planted her lips on mine.

She had nice lips.

Full and sweet.

I tasted the remnants of her fruity lip gloss, and the smell of
her shampoo filled my nostrils. She pressed her body
against mine. The uniform and the duty belts made things a
little clunky, but I figured those were temporary obstacles.

We melted into one another and released a lot of pent-up
tension.

The elevator lifted us skyward. The bell dinged when we hit her floor, and the doors slid open.

Connor was there to greet us. "You son-of-a-bitch!"

He cocked his fist back, stepped into the elevator, and swung as hard as he could.

Dakota and I broke apart, and I dodged the blow. He smacked the metal wall of the elevator, rumbling the paneling.

I grabbed his arm and wrenched it behind his back and shoved him against the wall. I twisted his hand up between his scapula, and he groaned in pain.

"What are you doing here?" Dakota growled.

"I came by to see you. To see if we could work things out."

"I told you. It's over. There is no working anything out."

"I knew there was something going on between you two," Connor growled.

"There was nothing going on between us until things ended." Dakota assured.

I kept him pressed against the wall. He wasn't going anywhere. I was just short of snapping something.

"Go home, Connor," she said.

"I just wanted to talk about things."

"There's nothing left to talk about. In case you hadn't heard, your business partner's in jail. Looks like he's going down for conspiracy to commit murder. And if I find out that you knew about the negligence beforehand and didn't say anything, I won't hesitate to come after you."

There was a long, tense moment.

"If I let you go, are you gonna cause trouble?" I asked.

Connor didn't say anything.

I pushed his arm a little bit farther to drive the point home.

He grimaced. "Okay. Enough!"

Dakota stepped off the elevator.

I backed away and cautiously let go.

Connor rubbed his shoulder and glared at me while I stepped off the elevator. The door slid shut, and the elevator descended.

Dakota and I exchanged a look.

"Well, that was awkward," she said.

She moved past me and walked down the hall.

I followed.

She dug into her pocket, and her keys jingled as she unlocked the door. She pushed it open and stepped inside, holding the door for me. "Welcome to my casa."

It was a nice place. Gray hardwoods, stylish furniture, a fireplace, a large terrace with a barbecue grill, and a view of the slopes. Marble countertops and stainless steel appliances in the kitchen. Sleek fixtures and elegant contemporary art on the walls.

"Before you ask, yes, I get a housing subsidy. I couldn't afford this place on my salary without it." Then she added, "We can't all be movie stars and pop idols."

"Is somebody jealous?"

"I'm not jealous of anyone or anything," she assured. "Want a drink?"

"Sure."

She peeled off her coat and tossed it on the sofa, then stepped to the mini bar and poured me a glass of whiskey. The fine amber liquid crackled and popped the cubes of ice. She grabbed a beer from the fridge, popped the top with a hiss, and we toasted. "Never a dull moment."

"Ain't that the truth."

She took a sip of her drink and exhaled the tension from her body. "Why do you always come into town and turn my life upside down?"

"I didn't turn your life upside down. I have no control over the Universe."

She gave me an uncertain glance and inched closer. "Where were we?"

"I still think this is too soon for you."

She laughed. "Since when are you the type to put on the brakes?"

"I'm just looking out for a friend. I wouldn't want to take advantage of the situation."

She laughed again, took another sip of her beverage, and set it on the counter. Dakota took off her duty belt. She unclasped her uniform, button by button, and lifted a sassy eyebrow. "Maybe I'm the one taking advantage of you."

Her delicate fingers peeled the blouse away. With a quick snap, she unbuttoned her bra, and the lacy fabric went slack. She slipped it from her shoulders, and her buoyant peaks jiggled. She put her hands on her hips and shifted onto one leg. "Are you really going to turn this down?"

50

I let her take advantage of me.

Again, and again.

We tumbled around the sheets and worked out a lot of that pent-up energy. When it was all said and done, we collapsed beside each other, a sweaty mess. Hearts beating, blood pumping, pleasure chemicals swirling.

"I forgot how much fun it was," she said, snuggling close.

"It's been a while."

"Maybe we should see each other more than once a year."

"Maybe we should."

I drifted off to sleep with her beside me and woke in the morning to the smell of bacon and eggs. I pulled myself out of bed and joined Dakota in the kitchen. I grabbed a cup of coffee and took a seat at the bar counter while she grilled.

"I've got bad news," she said. "You want to hear it?"

"I'm not sure. How bad is it?"

"Well, Dalton is out, and the charges have been dropped."

I lifted a surprised brow. "What!?"

"It seems Trevor had a change of heart and is saying his confession was coerced. That he had no choice but to tell you what you wanted to hear. The judge said that recording is inadmissible. I'm not going to say I told you so, but..."

"So Dalton's gonna walk away?" I groaned.

"For the time being. Unless we can find evidence to tie him directly to the crimes, it's business as usual." She sighed. "I'm going to get him on criminal negligence. I'm not exactly sure how, but..."

She seemed to be taking it all in stride.

We had a nice breakfast, then I used her computer to mock up some flyers. In bold font across the top of the page, it read: MISSING, with a picture of Amaryllis below.

We headed to the station, printed out a couple hundred copies, then hit Main Street, putting them up in store windows and handing them out to people on the street.

The search and rescue team was still out at Falcon Ridge, sweeping the area, but they were about to call it off.

I was still holding out hope.

We spent most of the day tacking up flyers everywhere—grocery stores, apartment complexes, condos, you name it.

We grabbed lunch at *Prospect Place*. Dakota's phone buzzed during the meal.

"Tell me something good," she said. Dakota listened intently, and a grim frown tugged her face. "Thanks for the update."

She ended the call and looked at me. "You're not going to like this. The feds are suspending the search. According to the cold exposure models, they don't think..."

She didn't want to say it, but in these temperatures with no shelter, food, or water, there was no way a young child could survive the elements.

It was a grim reality that I would have to face.

"My department will keep up the search as long as need be," Dakota said. "I just want to set expectations."

I nodded.

We finished lunch, and I picked up the tab.

We'd run out of flyers and were heading back to the station to print more when I got a call from an unknown number.

I answered, "Hello?"

"I have Amaryllis," a woman said in a shaky voice.

She had my undivided attention.

"I didn't know she was kidnapped. You have to believe me. Huck gave her to me to watch and said he'd pay me 20 grand. I've had her for a couple days. I just didn't know what to do."

"Just give her back, no questions asked. All I care about is getting Amaryllis back to her mother safe and sound. Is she okay?"

"She's fine."

"Where are you? I'll come to you."

"I just left her at the homeless shelter five minutes ago. Sorry." She ended the call.

I told Dakota, and she spun the vehicle around and flicked on the lights. The sirens howled. We sped to the shelter, double parked at the entrance, and hustled inside.

Amaryllis was with a staff member. "This woman just left her here," she said, almost in shock.

I knelt down beside the adorable little girl and smiled. A wave of relief washed over me. "I'm your uncle Tyson, and this is Sheriff Skye," I said in a soothing voice. "We're gonna take you home to your mom."

She nodded.

I opened my arms, and she ran to me and flung her arms around my neck as I scooped her up.

I asked Dakota to call Madison. She wouldn't answer my calls.

Within minutes, Madison arrived at the shelter and rushed into the lobby. Her face filled with wonder when she saw Amaryllis in my arms. She rushed to take her from me and held her tight. Tears of joy streamed down her cheeks. "Oh my God, Baby! Are you okay?"

Amaryllis nodded.

Madison looked like she was never going to let go, and I didn't blame her.

51

I took the stage at Silver Rush, the blinding spotlight beaming down on me. I couldn't see the audience from the glare. I shouted my usual phrase into the microphone. "Please welcome to the stage, the mighty... Wild Fury!"

The crowd went wild, and Dizzy struck a power cord as the band rushed onto the stage. I made my exit as they took their places, and JD screamed into the microphone, "Good evening, Alpine Park!"

We'd played the venue once before, and it was nice to be back on stage. Apparently, we'd made a lot of fans the last time we were here. The place was packed.

All was almost right with the world. Amaryllis was reunited with her mother, and we brought down a few perps but still had one more to go.

Styxx stomped the kick drum, and Crash thundered on bass. Wild Fury hit the audience like a freight train, bringing their brand of party rock to the small mountain town.

We stayed in Alpine Park for Christmas and celebrated at Madison's place. She had time to collect her thoughts on everything and was speaking to me again. For that, I was thankful.

We enjoyed good food, good drinks, and exchanged gifts around the tree. JD and I lavished presents on Amaryllis, but she was the best gift of all. Alive and unharmed.

There was more wrapping paper on the floor when it was all said and done than you could imagine. We probably went a little overboard, but it's an uncle's job to spoil the hell out of his niece.

JD and I pitched in and bought Dizzy a new custom guitar to replace the one that had been stolen. Months of trying to track it down had been fruitless. We'd contacted the builder and had an exact duplicate made—a stealth black finish, jumbo stainless steel frets, a slim neck, and a headstock shaped like a viper.

Dakota joined us for the festivities.

Madison gave me a card that brought a tear to my eye. She scribbled a handwritten note: *I'm glad you're my brother.*

It wasn't a novel, but it was enough. We gave each other a hug, and she whispered in my ear, "You'll come back next Christmas, won't you?"

"Absolutely."

"Amaryllis needs her uncle in her life."

I smiled, and my heart felt good. I may have misted up a bit.

Dakota's phone buzzed with a call, and she excused herself to take it. She had an intense conversation in the kitchen, then returned to the living room with a slight smirk on her lips. "Xavier Pratt wants to cut a deal. Says he's willing to testify against Dalton. Looks like justice will be served after all."

It would take a while to sort out all the details, but I was confident Dalton would pay for his crimes.

JD said, "I was thinking tomorrow we can go look at a few places."

I gave him a confused look.

"I've been checking out the local listings. There are some nice places up for sale right now. We could use a winter retreat."

I laughed.

"I'm serious. We could rent it out for big dollars during the season. And land around here isn't getting any cheaper. That's what I call a smart investment."

"Let's take a look," I said.

I called everyone back in Coconut Key and wished them a Merry Christmas. I promised we'd all get together on the boat and celebrate when we got back.

I was a little surprised when Sheriff Daniels said, "I have to admit, it's been a little odd without you two around. This is the longest you've been away from the island in quite a while."

"So, you're saying you miss us?"

"I wouldn't go that far, but you two need to get your asses back here."

"What's going on?"

"Well, that's what you're going to figure out when you get here."

Madison shouted from another room. "Tyson! Can you come here?"

Her tone sounded somewhat urgent. I excused myself, ended the call, and hustled through the house, following the sound of her voice to the bedroom. She'd discovered another secret panel in the wall. Behind it was another safe exactly like the one in the office. I'm guessing Quentin didn't know about this one. It didn't take much work to break in.

Inside—the sparkling Diamond Lion bracelet.

Covered in glittering diamonds with emeralds for eyes, the hypnotic bracelet drew wondrous stares from us all.

"What the hell am I going to do with this thing?" Madison asked.

JD and I shrugged.

"I know what I'd do," Jack muttered.

Ready for more?

The adventure continues with Wild Execution!

Join my newsletter and find out what happens next!

AUTHOR'S NOTE

Thanks for taking this incredible journey with me. I'm having such a blast writing about Tyson and JD, and I've got plenty more adventures to come. I hope you'll stick around for the wild ride.

Thanks for all the great reviews and kind words!

If you liked this book, let me know with a review on Amazon.

Thanks for reading!

—Tripp

TYSON WILD

Wild Ocean

Wild Justice

Wild Rivera

Wild Tide

Wild Rain

Wild Captive

Wild Killer

Wild Honor

Wild Gold

Wild Case

Wild Crown

Wild Break

Wild Fury

Wild Surge

Wild Impact

Wild L.A.

Wild High

Wild Abyss

Wild Life

Wild Spirit

Wild Thunder

Wild Season

Wild Rage

Wild Heart

Wild Spring

Wild Outlaw

Wild Revenge

Wild Secret

Wild Envy

Wild Surf

Wild Venom

Wild Island

Wild Demon

Wild Blue

Wild Lights

Wild Target

Wild Jewel

Wild Greed

Wild Sky

Wild Storm

Wild Bay

Wild Chaos

Wild Cruise

Wild Catch

Wild Encounter

Wild Blood

Wild Vice

Wild Winter

Wild Malice

Wild Fire

Wild Deceit

Wild Massacre

Wild Illusion

Wild Mermaid

Wild Star

Wild Skin

Wild Prodigy

Wild Sport

Wild Hex

Wild West

Wild Alpine

Wild Execution

Wild...

CONNECT WITH ME

I'm just a geek who loves to write. Follow me on Facebook.

Made in the USA
Columbia, SC
22 November 2024

47338522R00167